BULLY FOR YOU

The Darkness at Fall's Creek

Hot Off the Press

Chasing Charlie

K.V ROSE, KORI BLUE & RAVEN MCALLAN

Bully for You
ISBN # 978-1-83943-880-6
©Copyright K.V. Rose, Kori Blue & Raven McAllan 2020
Cover Art by Claire Siemaszkiewicz ©Copyright March 2020
Interior text design by Claire Siemaszkiewicz
Totally Bound Publishing

THE DARKNESS
AT FALL'S CREEK

Dedication

To anyone who ever fought past fear to find
something stronger to hold on to.

Chapter One

I was the only one in the entire jock-filled classroom dressed in black. There was a sea of orange and blue — Caven University's school colors — and a few boys in blue-gray sweats and white, fitted V-necks.

But I was the only one in black.

And, probably, the only one here who wasn't planning to go on to play a professional sport or fall back on Daddy's dream of law school.

I didn't have a daddy.

I had no intention of going to grad school.

And my hand-eye coordination meant the only sport I was okay with was running, and that was just to stay in shape.

Thankfully, the lecturer dismissed sports psychology early, and I threw my notebook into my bag and stood, ready to get the hell out of there. It was Halloween night. How no one here in this bubble of testosterone and sweat could respect that with appropriate colors was beyond me.

"You dropped something." *Fuck.*

I looked up, startled, and stopped trying to edge my way out of the stadium-style seats. A boy in a gray hoodie and dark blue shorts blocked my path.

"What?" I asked, confused, hefting my backpack higher on one shoulder.

The room was emptying and I wanted to get back to my dorm to prepare for horror movie night with my best friend, Holland.

The boy smirked.

"A pencil," he said, jerking his chin to indicate the floor. I glanced down, and saw that I had, in fact, dropped my mechanical pencil on the floor. Black, like my ripped jeans and hoodie.

I bent down to pick it up, but, right before I did, the boy's dark blue Adidas landed on it with a crack.

I jerked back, my face heating as I met his gaze.

He had hazel eyes, brown hair shaved on the sides and longer on top, and he was nearly a foot taller than me.

"What the fuck?" I spat, angry.

I heard laughter behind me and turned to glance over my shoulder. A small group of Caven's cheerleaders and—I assumed, based on their shorts and jerseys—basketball players were watching us in amusement.

I turned back to the boy.

He was smiling, but it was anything but friendly.

"Why're you in this class, Freckles?"

I was positive my face—and freckles—were a shade of tomato red. I didn't bother to tell him my name was Aria.

He moved his foot. I looked down at the pencil. It was broken in two. Useless.

I turned around to go out the other way through the aisle, even though it meant I'd have to walk past the group of asshole jocks down below.

But just as I took a step, I was yanked backward and almost fell on my ass. It was only Hazel Eyes who

8

stopped me, his hands clutching my forearms to keep me from falling. He spun me around and let go of me, his eyes staring into mine.

"Watch it," he warned. "I wouldn't want to break you too."

There was no more laughter at my back. He'd said those words just for me to hear. Before I could say anything else — not that I had any idea what to say at all — he turned around and went down the steps to meet his friends at the door. He didn't glance back at me once.

I picked up the two halves of my broken pencil and stuffed them in my hoodie pockets.

* * * *

Holland was waiting in my dorm when I let myself in, propped up on his elbows on my lofted bed. He looked up from whatever fantasy novel he'd been engrossed in and frowned.

"What happened?" he asked at once, and I tossed my bag in my shoebox-sized closet and collapsed into the beanbag chair in the corner of my private room.

Private, because I had a scholarship that let me afford it. And because the thought of sharing a cramped space with a stranger made me feel panicky.

I ran a hand through my long hair — pale pink this week — and twirled a strand around my finger. A nervous habit.

"Nothing," I mumbled as Holland sat up, his skinny, pale legs hanging off the bed.

He adjusted his glasses and narrowed his eyes, the book closed beside him on my gray comforter, a sheet of paper he used as a bookmark poking out between the pages.

"Stop lying, A." He crossed his arms over his chest, black Ozzy T-shirt peeking through them.

I glanced at the white ceiling, the dim light that I could have sworn buzzed overhead. I never complained about it, but now it grated on my nerves. I was lucky, I knew, to be alone.

Although sometimes it didn't feel that way.

I glanced out of the window, my silver, thrifted curtains opened wide. Evening was coming, and I saw at least two students carrying pumpkins as they walked along Caven's brick pathways.

"Some idiot in sports psych," I said, shaking my head, trying to clear my mind. It didn't matter. I met Holland's baby-blue eyes and offered him a smile. "Wanna get a PSL?" I asked, arching a brow.

That got him laughing. Pumpkin spice lattes were *not* Holland's thing. He rolled his eyes, adjusted his glasses and shook his head, blond curls bouncing as he did. I always thought Holland was my own personal guardian angel, sent to me in kindergarten after my parents got divorced and Dad moved too far away. They'd worked things out, got back together, but Holland had never left. Not even after Dad went so far away, I'd never reach him again. Holland was by my side at his funeral.

And here we were, sophomores at Caven together. The blond hair and blue eyes only added to his angel persona.

"You are one basic bitch," he said with a grin.

I rolled my eyes. "What a sweetheart."

He hopped down from my bed and offered me his hand. I took it, and he pulled me to my feet.

We left my room together after I darted a quick glance at my reflection in the long mirror that hung on my dorm room door—pale pink waves, shadows under green eyes and skinny arms and limbs that even my hoodie couldn't hide.

Everything about my appearance screamed 'English major,' and up until an asshole jock had broken my mechanical pencil moments ago, I hadn't cared. Now, I felt strange in my own skin.

"Why are you even in a sports class?" Holland asked as we took the steps down from my dorm two at a time.

We didn't even have to fight our way through a crowd for once. Caven was in one of the smallest towns in all of Virginia, just outside of Roanoke. Which meant for holidays—Halloween included—the cool kids usually went elsewhere.

But Holland and I had never been cool kids.

When we pushed open the double doors and I felt the crisp, cool wave of fall wash over us, I let the memory of the jerk fade away.

"I needed a psych class. It was the only one I could get in when it came time to register."

Holland snorted. "You could've taken it next semester. Hell, you could've taken it next year."

I pinched his arm, still threaded through mine. "I like to plan ahead," I said with a wink.

He hissed, swearing under his breath, and I threw my head back and laughed.

"After PSLs," he said, voice low, "there's somewhere I want to take you."

I met his gaze after we crossed the empty street outside of my dorm, to the little strip mall with the independent coffee shop that usually had a line out through the door.

No such line today.

"Where?" I asked, my stomach fluttering. I hated surprises. "I thought we were watching *The Witch*—"

"We are," he cut me off, and disentangled his arm from mine as he grabbed the door to Cups. He jerked his head, gesturing for me to go ahead. The smell of coffee and the sound of espresso machines beckoned me in like a siren's call. "But we're going to check out a haunted house first."

Chapter Two

"All right, A, who do I need to punch?" Holland asked in a low voice. We were tucked into a booth in the corner of Cups, only a handful of students and professors scattered about the sleek coffee shop.

I shook my head, looked down at my plastic cup. I took a sip of an iced, half-sweet PSL. I had pulled my hood up, slouched down low in the booth.

"Aria Rosen, what the fuck is wrong with you?" Holland prodded again, scowling at me.

I felt my cheeks grow pink but kept my head down. And because I knew Holland was absolutely horrible at taking hints, I mumbled under my breath, "The guy ordering right now broke my pencil today."

Holland let out a low breath, his pale fingers dug into his Styrofoam cup. I saw, out of the corner of my eye, that he turned and glanced at the jerk, who stood in front of three other basketball players, his back to us. With an attitude like his, combined with his height and his posse, he had to be a basketball player.

Or something.

Thankfully, Holland didn't stare. He turned back around to face me, and I kept my head down.

"On purpose?" he asked, his voice quiet.

I nodded, shame burning through me.

I was an English major, Holland was fine arts. We didn't get bullied much, not here in college. Those days were behind us, or so we thought. In college, like gravitated to like. And while neither of us had many friends, we didn't have many enemies either.

But that was, apparently, before I did something stupid like take sports psychology.

"Don't worry about him," Holland said in a low voice, reaching across the table to grab my hand. But he yanked it back as if I'd burned him. "Damn, you need to stop getting iced drinks—your fingers are freezing!" He shook out his hand, sucked on his fingers.

I rolled my eyes. Drama queen. "I hate hot coffee." Not something I needed to point out to him.

Holland opened his mouth to respond—probably to defend his own hot cup of PSL—when he stopped short, his mouth snapping closed, and eyes narrowed.

I frowned, looked in the direction he was gazing.

Then my stomach sank.

It was the same boy who had broken my pencil.

His full lips curved in a devious smile. He had sharp cheekbones, and light, golden skin. I'd been too flustered earlier to notice, but he was beautiful.

Which made what he said next all the more cruel. "Ah, and so the trash takes itself out together."

I knew he was referring to Holland too, but he kept his eyes on me, the wooden backing of the booth the only thing separating us.

"What was that you were saying," he asked, feigning politeness, "about hot coffee?"

He held a large, Styrofoam cup in his own long-fingered hands. Beyond him, seated at stools that faced a window with a view of the parking lot, were his three friends. They were watching us, taking sips from their own cups, smirks on their faces.

I didn't answer him.

"Don't you have something better to do?" Holland challenged him, anger lacing his words.

The boy's brown-green eyes flicked to Holland, that same cruel smile on his beautiful face. He didn't say a single thing to him, only stared him down, his expression one of cold, calm malice. I didn't have to look at Holland to know that even he was shrinking from this boy's gaze.

Beyond him, one of his friends slid down from his stool.

"Ready, Dante?" he called.

Dante. Of course his name would be something like Dante. I gripped the cold cup in my hands tighter, condensation slick against my fingers.

Dante held up his coffee cup, and for one horrifying moment, I thought he was going to throw it at me.

"I'm not done here," he said. I knew he was talking to his friend, even though he neither looked at the guy, nor raised his voice.

He was the leader of the four of them.

That much was clear.

He angled his cup down, as if he were going to pour the hot coffee over me. I sucked in a breath, but I couldn't move. My limbs seemed frozen in place, my chest tight.

But then he stopped, the cup tilted between us, his hand steady.

"I'm not going to burn you, Freckles," he said in a low voice. "Not yet."

Then he turned around and walked out of the door, his friends following behind, shooting glares in my direction. As if I had just threatened them with hot coffee.

I exhaled and realized I had been holding my breath throughout the whole encounter. Slowly, I turned to face Holland.

His face was even whiter than usual.

"What. The. Fuck just happened?"

I shook my head, and realized my heart was hammering in my chest. "He clearly doesn't want me in his psychology class," I muttered.

"Do you know who that is?" Holland's tone made me look up.

I pulled my hood from my hair and shook my head.

Holland's eyes widened. "He's like...he's like a god at Caven. Dante Llera. He's the star quarterback on the basketball team—"

"Pretty sure there's no quarterback in basketball," I interrupted.

Holland gestured vaguely with his hand, brushing my remark aside. "Whatever. He's a senior. Supposedly going to the NBA when he graduates. The dude is a legend. His family owns most of Fall's Creek. Roanoke too."

I blinked. Once. Twice. I shook my head. Opened my mouth. Closed it. Because surely my best friend, fantasy nerd and art aficionado, wasn't actually defending an asshole who had humiliated me not once, but twice, for no apparent reason. All because this guy played basketball.

Holland didn't even like basketball.

He must've seen the look on my face. He shook his head, licked his lips. "No, no, no, no, no," he said quickly. "He's a real asshole. Clearly." He waved his hand in my direction as if I was Dante's exhibit A in being an asshole. "I'm just... Why is he tormenting you? I'm confused."

I threw up my hands. "Fuck if I know! I told you, he broke my pencil in psych, and then said something about breaking me" — my face heated with those words — "and then he shows up here. And, well" — I shook my head — "you saw what he did."

Holland took a sip of his coffee and leaned back in the booth. "Forget about him. Complete dick."

We sat in silence for a few moments as the coffee shop emptied out. Halloween was my favorite time of year. I should've been excited. I had been excited, even after the broken pencil incident. But now...now I felt kind of numb.

Dante Llera had singlehandedly ruined my mood with a few cold words. And the worst part was I couldn't get his stupid hazel eyes out of my head.

Fuck this. I stood to my feet, drained the rest of my iced latte in one gulp, and tossed it into the trash behind the booth.

"Let's go."

Holland pushed to his feet and arched a blond brow. "Where to?" he asked, hesitant. I knew what he was thinking. Maybe I just wanted to hole up with him in my dorm room.

But fuck that, too.

I was twenty years old. I was in college on a full-ride scholarship, which meant the money I made working part-time at the library was mine to spend on what I wanted. I would be damned if some arrogant jock was going to ruin my favorite night of the year.

I thought of Mom, working nights scrubbing commercial toilets to make ends meet, ever since Dad died. She would be pissed if she knew I'd spent the night sulking and pouting over a dickhead.

I met Holland's gaze.

"Take me to the haunted house," I said, shrugging. "Let's see if you can scare me again."

Chapter Three

We headed down the side street adjacent to Cups. Away from Caven, away from the small-town core of Fall's Creek. We had lived in Fall's Creek most of our lives, and yet every time we walked this stretch of the town, I felt the hairs on the nape of my neck stand on end.

The Fall's Creek cemetery was here, lining the sidewalk, a black iron fence separating us from the dilapidated tombstones on the other side. We had yet to see a single car pass us by since we started out.

The sun had set, few stars strewn across the dark sky. I wrapped my arms around myself and shivered.

"Scared already?" Holland teased at my side.

I shook my head.

Despite the lack of traffic, I could smell a bonfire in the air. We heard the whooping and hollering of some of the students who'd decided to celebrate Halloween at Caven after all.

"I don't recall a real haunted house in Fall's Creek," I said, testing the waters. The truth was, the town was full of haunted places. But over the years, Holland and I had meticulously crossed them all off our little list. We were amateur ghost hunters. We'd even been in the local paper a few years ago for all the places we'd braved our way into. And we had yet to see a ghost.

Holland flashed me a smile, his teeth visible in the dark surrounding us.

"The thing is, A, this place is new."

I frowned at that, risking a glance at the silent graveyard to my right. Towering trees cast strange shadows around the graves in the dim light of the crescent moon. I had no idea why I could handle pseudo-haunted houses, but not cemeteries. Another kink in my strange brain.

I forced myself to look ahead. A short stretch of road that ended in a wild, thick forest. I knew the homes that lined this street. Most of them were lived in.

"I thought haunted houses were...old. You know, because, for them to be haunted, people had to die there?"

Holland let out a huff of laughter. "Haven't you ever heard, Aria? The good die young."

I stuffed my hands into my hoodie pockets. It was growing chillier outside. "If they were good," I pressed, "they wouldn't haunt a house after they passed on."

Holland poked me in the ribs. "Always looking on the bright side."

I shrugged. That wasn't true, of course. My mind was wild. Thorny. Dark. But right now, beneath Halloween's dark sky, I was feeling nervous. Edgy. I chalked it up to Dante's bullying, and the fact that I hadn't 'ghost hunted' with Holland in years, since before college. Before Dad died.

Because after he did...I worried I'd see him every-where.

I guess Holland thought I was ready to try again.

He linked his arm through mine and smiled down at me. His bright blue eyes shone even in the dark. "It'll be fine, A," he reassured me.

I sighed but didn't argue. The wild forest of Fall's Creek was fast approaching, and we passed a few homes with lights on, some decorated for Halloween. We could hear engines revving in the distance, tires peeling from somewhere close to campus.

"Ah, if only I had an engine to gun," I said with a playful laugh. Neither Holland nor I owned a car. Mom and I had scrimped since Dad died. He had been the breadwinner in the family. Mom had taken care of me. Holland's parents owned a little bed and breakfast up the road, in an even smaller town than Fall's Creek. Needless to say, they didn't make much.

"If you had that much money, then maybe we wouldn't be so skinny," Holland joked.

"I wish I weren't so skinny." It was the truth. My boobs were basically nonexistent. My appearance was unique...because I dyed my hair every color under the sun. And generally speaking, I was okay to look at. But boys liked curves. I had none.

I'd dated, on and off, but never anything serious. And my sex life had been so-so since I started back in high school.

"Bitch, stop whining. Girls are literally throwing up their last meal to look like you. I don't want to hear it."

Before I could open my mouth to defend myself, Holland stopped, jerking me to a halt too.

We were at the edge of the forest.

I rounded on him, yanking my arm from his.

"I thought you said this was a new place!" I accused, flinging a finger to the woods. I was not stepping foot in there. Not in the middle of the night on Halloween. I'd rather be safe and sound in my dorm room, cuddled under my comforter and eating popcorn. The old me would have loved this place. The new me...not so much.

Holland made an impatient sound in his throat. "It is new. Down this path." He moved my outstretched finger until I was pointing at a small, paved driveway, snaking in between the dense woods. It was hard to make it out in the night, but there were small reflectors on either side of it. I hadn't noticed until now.

"What's down there?" I asked. Holland released my hand and I let it fall to my side. I wasn't ready to go trekking down that path.

Not until I had some answers.

"A house, Aria. Just a house."

"Why are we here if it's just a house?"

"It's a mansion. A glass and stone mansion. And the owners abruptly moved out, like, two weeks ago. My parents told me about it. They said it was haunted."

I shook my head, peering into the dark forest. I heard insects crawling in there. And beyond us, back toward Caven, the sound of life. The scent of a bonfire still lingered, even here. I relished in that. I had no friends to crowd around a bonfire with, but still, it meant there were flesh and blood people back there, back at Caven.

'I wouldn't want to break you too.'

Dante's words came back to me.

That was the kind of people back at Caven.

I squared my shoulders.

"That doesn't make sense, Holland. If it's a new house, why would they just...up and move?"

"Maybe they were the crazy ones. Or maybe they brought in a ghost." He took a step forward, leaving the asphalt for the cement driveway. He glanced over his shoulder at me. "Coming?"

"There's no For Sale sign," I pointed out.

He sighed, casting his gaze to the night sky. "Mom said it wasn't on the market yet. But it's definitely vacant. Let's go?" I saw him tilt his head in the darkness.

After a moment, I nodded. "Why not," I murmured, and followed after him.

* * * *

Everything was going fine.

Until it wasn't.

The driveway was long, and I was glued to Holland's side the entire walk up it. Or, rather, down it. It sloped down a hill, and I could make out nothing ahead of us as we walked. It was so dark here, beneath the thick canopy of trees overhead, that I wouldn't be able to see my own hand in front of my face.

Not that I tried to see it.

My hands were affixed to Holland's arm.

"I haven't gotten this much action in far too long," he joked. Normally, I would've shoved him away with that comment, but not now. Now, I clung tighter.

"Shut up," I said through clenched teeth.

Then, just when the mansion — and it was a mansion — came into view, we heard something scurry in the leaves beside us.

I froze, and even Holland was tense beneath my hands.

For a long moment, we didn't speak.

"What was that?" I whispered, my knees trembling beneath me.

I heard Holland swallow at my side. "Probably a squirrel," he managed to say, but even his voice shook.

I looked ahead, taking in the modern-day cabin, complete with a wide wall of floor-to-ceiling windows on the second floor, and a door made of stone. There were floodlights on the corners of the rectangular house. They were dim and didn't light the rest of the path ahead of us, but it was better than nothing.

Taking a deep breath, the two of us moved forward, pressing closer to the house. The driveway ended in front of a detached two-car garage, but we took the little stone walkway right up to the front door.

Only then did I dare to look back.

Nothing.

Just blackness as far as I could see.

We had walked a long way into this forest.

Panic clawed at me.

"Holland, maybe we should—"

There it was again.

Another rustling in the leaves. I could hear my heart pounding in my ears. It felt like the blood was draining from my head as panic seized me.

Before, I never had panic attacks. Before, I marched through haunted houses like I owned them.

But after...after Dad died...I had them all the time.

And one was coming.

Now.

Holland darted out his hand to the door, pressing down on the handle's lever. Surprising me, the door opened, and we hurried inside. Holland closed it behind us, and I smelled fresh paint, and something else too...something like flavored tobacco.

Unless the previous owners had vaped inside their house for hours on end, someone had been in here before us. My skin crawled at the thought as I blinked, trying to take in the interior of the house, letting my eyes adjust. It was silent inside. I could hear my blood pounding in my ears, but even so, the panic attack edged away, my pulse slowing with it.

Then, right beside me, Holland screamed.

"Run!" he yelled, terror lining his words. "RUN!"

I tried to reach for him, to find his arm in the darkness. But, before I could, before I could move at all, someone grabbed me, putting a hand over my mouth.

And in my ear Dante whispered, "Hello, Freckles. I've been waiting for you."

Chapter Four

Dante's hand on my mouth should have made me panic.

Instead, I quieted.

He pulled me away from the door, one arm wrapped around my chest, pinning my arms to my sides, the other still over my mouth. I heard laughter somewhere beyond us.

"Careful," he said in my ear, his breath caressing my skin. He smelled like mint and tobacco, a heady combination that made me relax, just a little, into his arms.

There were more voices, but I couldn't make out the words as we ascended the stairs.

I wanted to find Holland, but I didn't dare move. Dante had at least a foot in height over me, and his grip was strong. I didn't need to know he was a college athlete destined to go pro to know he was stronger than I was.

When we got to the top of the stairs, he pulled me into a room, released me and shut the door after us.

It was hard to see him in the darkness of the room, but I rounded on him all the same.

"What the hell is happening?" I asked, my words coming out in gasps. My heart was flying in my chest, my breathing shallow. The panic was coming back.

He moved in front of me, his hands running down my arms. I was glad I had on a hoodie. Glad I couldn't feel his skin on mine. I could still smell him, and that was almost too much.

"Shh," he said, "you're having a panic attack."

At that, I stilled.

I was having a panic attack. Or at least, I was on the verge of one.

But how would he know that?

He didn't know me.

I made it a point to keep my head down in sports psychology, and he had never spoken to me before today.

I took a step back from him. Or, rather, I tried to, but he gripped my arms tighter.

"Don't move," he said, his words a command. "Stay close to me."

I tried to laugh, but it came out all wrong. "What is happening?" I asked again, trying to slow my breathing. "Where is Holland?"

There was a stretch of silence between us, his hands still gripping my arms. I could make out his hazel eyes in the darkness, my eyes adjusting. My breathing started to steady itself. The panic was slipping away, a little at a time.

It made no sense.

"Your friend is safe," Dante answered me.

And me? I wanted to ask, but I couldn't form the words.

He let go of me, and for one strange moment, I wished he hadn't.

But then he was behind me. I could feel his body heat against me, and he didn't touch me as he leaned down over me, his lips brushing my neck as he spoke. "Do you like to be scared, Aria?"

Aria.

He knew my name.

Why that mattered, I didn't know. It shouldn't have mattered. I should have been screaming. I should have been running.

But his question...

I did like to be scared. I'd always like to be scared. I hated surprises, but I loved the fear of the unknown. It pushed me to my edge. Before Dad died, I'd been an outcast just as I was now. But I had been a free one—I'd skydived for my sixteenth birthday—also documented in Fall's Creek's newspaper. I'd gotten high on whipped-cream cans in the middle of the night with Holland after his parents had gone to bed. I'd marched into every haunted location in Fall's Creek with no fear. Or, rather, with a hell of a lot of bravery.

I'd liked the thrill of it.

All that had gone away after Dad passed.

"I asked you a question, Aria." There was a command in his voice that felt twisted. Wrong.

I liked it.

"Yes," I finally managed to say. "Yes."

"Yes what?" he pressed, his lips still hovering above my neck. He pulled my hair away, draping it over one shoulder, exposing my skin to him. A chill went down my spine.

"Yes," I said again. "I like to be scared."

Then I heard something, beyond the closed door of our room.

For a moment, my chest tightened as I thought of Holland. I had no idea where he was. I was going on Dante's word that he was safe, but I didn't know Dante. The only two interactions we'd had before this, he'd tried to intimidate me.

He had intimidated me.

But then my face heated when I realized what the sound was.

Moaning.

A girl's moan, breathy and loud. It seemed to be coming from down the hall.

"What is that?" I asked, my voice shaking with the words.

I felt Dante smile against my skin. His arms encircled me, pressing me to him.

"I think you know what that is, Aria. You're not so innocent, are you?"

My mouth was dry, and my head was spinning. I didn't answer him. I didn't know what to say. The woman's moan grew louder, and I heard something else too. A man's rumbled words. Words I couldn't quite catch, and I was glad of it.

"Who is it?" I asked.

"Does it matter?" Dante countered. After a moment of us standing together like that, my back against his front, his arms pressed tight around me, he asked, "Do you want to go watch?"

My instinct was to say no. But I realized, as my mouth tried to form the word…it was a lie.

That thrill was coming back. That fear. Because this was all kinds of wrong. And yet…

I nodded, knowing he wouldn't see me in the dark.

But he must have felt it. He started to move with me.

"Holland," I said again, forcing my thoughts from the warmth spooling in my core. From how my body felt against Dante's. From the sound of the two people having sex just outside of these walls.

"I told you, he'll be safe."

That was all Dante was going to give me for now.

And it might have made me a horrible friend, but I took it, and didn't ask again.

Dante took my hand, his engulfing my own, and tugged me out of the room and down the hall, closer to the sound of moaning, of skin slapping against skin. I was thankful for the darkness—my face was so hot, I thought I was burning up from the inside out. But I let Dante pull me along, my feet stumbling every few steps.

It was warm inside the house, despite the cool fall outside. Like these rooms had been shut closed for far too long. There was sweat on my brow, but I didn't dare wipe it off. There was something I liked about this…the danger, the slickness, Dante's hand in mine.

It was stupid.

It was dangerous.

But I didn't care.

We stopped walking, the moans the loudest here, and people talking, whispering, laughing. Dante pushed open a door—I heard the faint creak of it.

Then he pulled me into the room.

The door clicked closed behind us.

For a moment, I stood rooted to the spot, staring.

The crowd gathered in here had grown quiet with our arrival. The only sound that hadn't changed was that of the woman enjoying herself in front of a feral audience. She was still moaning, breathy words intermingled in between her cries of pleasure. "God, that feels so good. Don't stop."

It smelled like sex in here.

Like fear too.

And like someone was vaping. I saw clouds of smoke above the crowd's heads.

I drank it all in.

"Look who Dante dragged along," a guy said ahead of me, a low whistle after his words.

It wasn't my imagination that felt Dante's hand tighten around my own.

I forced myself to really look, and I saw a dozen pairs of eyes on me. Every single one of the people in here, save for the ones in the middle of the circle, had wicked smiles on their faces.

There were boys and girls, some holding cans of beer, others with red cups. Some were vaping, clouds of smoke filling the room then dissipating. And there was a lamp in here, tucked away in a corner. It didn't give much light, but it was enough.

I recognized some of the boys. They had been with Dante at Cups.

Holland wasn't here.

I forced my eyes away from them, to the center of the ring.

My eyes widened, my breath catching in my throat.

Dante pulled me closer to his side, and people made way for him in the circle.

I had been wrong.

It wasn't two people having sex.

It was three.

The girl had her head thrown back, long, blonde hair tumbling down to her waist. She cried out in pleasure, but I felt certain there was a little pain there too. A guy was holding her up, her legs wrapped around his waist, his hands spreading her ass apart. Behind her, another guy was in her ass, and he had a fistful of her hair in his fingers, yanking her head back.

The three of them moved in tandem, and I saw sweat drip down their skin. I watched each of the boys slam their cocks to the hilt in the girl, who took it with low moans, her fingers digging into the guy's back in front of her.

Dante leaned down, his fingers still entwined in mine.

"Do you like to watch?" His cool breath caressed the shell of my ear.

I couldn't look away, which I guessed was answer enough.

"Of course she does," the same boy who had spoken when we walked in said from beside Dante. He was one of those from the coffee shop. He had thick blond hair, a red cup in his hand, basketball shorts hung low on his hips. He wasn't wearing a shirt. "Who doesn't?" He winked at me, and Dante turned to stare at him.

"Lay off her, Scott."

The boy called Scott scoffed, just in time to the girl in the center crying out someone's name—Jackson.

Scott grinned at the sound, but his eyes were steady on mine.

"Look, Dante, I know you've always had a thing for this little goth girl..." He left the circle and walked around to my side, leaning down close to me. "But we can share her." His dark eyes flicked up to Dante, at my back. "That's what teammates are for, right, Dante?"

Dante released my hand, and instead brought his own to the small of my back. His fingertips dug in, just a little. "Tell him," he said in my ear, but loud enough for Scott to hear.

People were talking around us, and the girl's moans had turned into labored sighs. They seemed to be almost done, but I didn't dare look as I held Scott's gaze.

I shook my head. "Tell him what?" I asked, my voice quiet.

Dante's fingers dug into my back a little more.

"Tell him who you belong to."

A shiver went down my spine at his words. I shook my head, my face heating all over again. But I didn't want Scott to keep looking at me like that. And as Dante's hands trailed from my back to around my waist, tugging me flush against him, all rational thought went out of the window.

"I'm his," I said, and Dante pulled me closer.

"You heard her," he said in that same quiet voice, "so get the fuck away from her."

Scott looked up to Dante, frowned, but then he turned around and found a place for himself further down from us in the middle of the circle.

The slapping sounds of skin on skin had stopped, and I could only hear heavy breathing in the center of the circle.

"Do you want a turn?" Dante asked in my ear, before I could look at what was happening.

I shook my head.

He dipped his head, mouth against my neck. "Right answer," he said, and he put his arm around my shoulders and steered me toward the door without telling anyone goodbye. When we had left the room, he pulled the door closed, and pushed me against the wall, hands on either side of my head, caging me in.

His eyes were on my mouth.

"Are you scared?" he asked.

I blinked, eyes widening. "I...I don't know," I admitted. It was true enough.

He trailed one finger down my check, over my collarbone. "Take this off," he commanded, tugging on the strings of my hoodie.

I had only a tank top underneath.

I shook my head.

A smile played on his lips. "Aria," he said calmly, "take this off." He bit his lip, tilting his head, as if considering something, even though I hadn't said a word. "Or would you rather I do it?"

I rubbed my hands along my thighs, nervous. His eyes followed that gesture, and his dimples flashed, lips twisting up in amusement.

Both of his hands came to the edges of my hoodie, fingers skimming along my skin beneath. The crowd on the other side of the door was talking loudly, and it seemed the sex show was over. Any minute, they were going to spill out into the hallway and see us, Dante and me.

He lifted my hoodie, his motions tentative, as if waiting to see if I would stop him.

But I didn't.

Then he pulled it over my head, reached around me, and tied it to my waist. Tight.

His eyes drank me in, lingering on my chest. I wanted to cover myself, but I fisted my hands at my sides. Instead, I let him have his fill. I could have sworn I heard him groan.

But he didn't touch me. Instead, he placed his hands back along the wall, on either side of me. He looked...hungry.

"What do you want from me?" I managed to ask, trying to think of Holland. Trying to think of how stupid this was. How ridiculous. Dante was an asshole. And more than that, there was nothing about him that should have wanted me. I was a nobody, a 'goth girl,' one with pale pink hair and chipped black nail polish. Dante was a basketball star, a rich kid that looked the part. He was…beautiful.

He shook his head at my question, eyes meeting mine. "How bad are you, Freckles?" he asked.

My face heated at the nickname. "I-I'm not," I said, throat feeling dry. I looked beyond him, at the darkness of the rest of the house. This was Halloween. I was supposed to be watching horror movies with Holland. Inside my dorm. Safe.

Bored, a little voice in my head whispered.

"Oh," Dante said, finger trailing down my throat, "I think you are." When he reached the top of my tank top, he stopped. He was studying me, to see if I would stop him.

I didn't.

He trained his fingers lower, gliding along my nipple through my shirt. I hardened at his touch and a rasp of laughter came from his beautiful mouth. He circled my nipple, toying with me. I arched into his touch, as if on instinct, my body craving his.

His hand cupped my breast, and he pressed his leg between mine. I pushed against him and he smiled, but there was no warmth in it.

He wound his other hand in my hair, fingers tugging on my strands.

"I like this color on you," he said as he gazed down at me, eyes dipping down to my hips pressing against him. Then he pulled me in front of him, pushing himself against the wall, my back pressed against him.

And I could feel just what I'd done to him.

His fingers went under my tank top, from the bottom, trailing up my stomach, making me shiver.

He bent his head, kissing my shoulder blade. "We fit perfectly like this, you and I," he said against my skin. Then he pressed himself into me and I pressed back, savoring the feel of the thick ridge through his basketball shorts. "Don't we, Aria?"

I fumbled for words. "You...you broke my pencil today," I said, hating the way my words came out weak, wrong.

He dragged his teeth along my shoulder, and I felt the wetness between my legs. His hands still danced along my stomach, but I wanted them lower.

"I wanted everyone to know," he said, his breath cool along my skin.

I exhaled, uneven and ragged. "Know what?"

He glided his tongue along my skin, using his teeth to pull at the thin strap of my tank top. It fell down my arm, and he nuzzled his lips against my bare skin. "Know that you're mine."

My core tightened at that, and his hands finally went lower, skimming the tops of my jeans.

Then the door opened beside us, people spilling out into the hallway.

He straightened behind me, placed his hands on either side of my hips, people passing us by, shooting us glances.

"Let's go," he said to me, and he pushed me away from him, made to take my hand and lead me down the hall.

I shook my head. "No," I said, planting my feet.

"Careful with her, Dante. She looks fragile," a guy said, clapping Dante on the back. Dante said nothing, only shrugged the guy's hand off him.

"No?" Dante asked me as people gathered in the hallway, some against the walls like we were, others going down the steps, some spilling into the other rooms. His voice sounded dangerous. Dark.

"No," I breathed, my heart nearly pounding out of my chest. I thought of Holland, of how he might kill me for this. But fuck it. He wanted me to live again. "I want you. Here."

"Do you?" Dante asked, amused. He gripped my arm, pulling me to him. I craned my neck back to take him in. "Not here." His tone was firm. "I don't want anyone else to see you." Then he yanked me down the stairs after him.

I didn't bother trying to resist.

Chapter Five

The woods were dark.

No one seemed to have come outside, and although I cast a glance around for Holland, I would never have been able to find him in the darkness. Dante pulled me up the long driveway, his steps hurried but even, and neither of us spoke.

Not at first.

I was trying to breathe. To think about all the reasons why I shouldn't do this. All the reasons I should pull away from him, find Holland, get the hell out of here.

But I couldn't do it.

So I followed him, hoping I wouldn't regret it.

And when someone jumped in front of us, from behind the trees lining the path, I thought I already did.

To my credit, I didn't scream, but that probably had more to do with the fact that I was finding it hard to breathe than because I was feeling brave.

Dante stopped, pushing me behind him.

Whoever it was started laughing. A guy's laughter. I couldn't see him from behind Dante.

"Dante, man, you should have seen your face—"

"Get out of here," Dante growled.

The hairs on my neck stood on end.

If I had been whoever he was talking to, I would have run. But the guy kept laughing.

"Who's that you got there?" he asked, seeming to notice me for the first time. He peered around Dante's shoulder. I could make out curly hair, the whites of his eyes, and not much else.

Dante shoved the guy back, out of my sight.

"I said, get out of here," he repeated, anger lining his words.

"Yo, chill. Don't you like to share your girls, bro?"

My gut tightened. No. He didn't seem as if he liked to share.

"She's mine." Those words again. They made me feel…shaky. Good.

"Sorry, man, sorry." The guy actually sounded sorry. I assumed it wasn't a good idea to piss off Dante Llera. "See you later," the guy mumbled and he walked around us, glancing back at me as he did so, then breaking out into a jog toward the house.

"Fucking idiot," Dante muttered.

I don't know what made me do it, but I let go of his hand, took his shoulders in my grasp and pushed him against the tree, my body pressing into his.

"You're so worried someone else wants me," I whispered, standing on my tippy toes, my mouth hovering over his. "But you won't take me, either. Maybe I'm better off…" I shot a deliberate glance toward the house. If he wanted to play, we could play. If I was going to get my guts back, I might as well go all out.

His body tensed beneath me, and he spun me around, switching our places, my back against the tree.

"I'm not letting you get away from me. There's nowhere for you to hide here. So, you can run, if you'd like." He took my wrists in one hand, pinned my arms over my head, and I saw in the darkness his gaze run up and down the length of my body. "But I'm not leaving you here."

I flashed him a shy smile. "Then do something about it."

He tilted his head. "About what?" he asked, eyes narrowed.

I bucked my hips, my arms still pinned over my head, and rubbed my core against his hard cock.

"About this."

He gave a soft laugh. "I'm not taking you in the woods, beautiful girl. I know you like to act tough"—he tugged a strand of my hair—"but I need more room than this to take what's mine."

* * * *

We made it back to the road. He led me to the closest driveway, and I saw a black Mercedes in front of a closed, two-car garage. Lights flashed on the car as he unlocked it.

He opened the passenger door and I slid inside.

He closed my door, got in and threw the car in reverse, backing out, engine growling.

"Put your seat belt on," he commanded.

I peered at the house he had parked in front of. It was two stories, white and cozy, but it definitely didn't look like the house of a family that owned most of Fall's Creek.

"Is this your house?" I asked.

"Seat belt," he said, throwing the car into gear and speeding down the road.

I rolled my eyes but did as he said. I glanced around the black leather interior—it was spotless.

"No," he said, answering my question. "A friend's."

I let out a little laugh. "One of your friends that wanted to fuck me tonight?"

He skidded the car to a stop in the middle of the deserted street, eyes narrowing on me. In the dashboard lights, I saw the green of his irises, the set of his jaw.

"None of my friends are going to fuck you," he said, brow arched. "No one else is going to fuck you from now on. Do you understand that?"

A smile curved on my lips. "We'll see," I teased.

He let out a low growl, then put his foot on the gas, heading toward Caven.

"How do you know me?" I asked as he drove on the deserted streets, the brick buildings of our university looming ahead. "I've never seen you before. Before today."

He didn't speak for a moment, driving through the roundabout.

When he did, his voice was low. "We had an art class together. Two years ago. Your freshman year."

I stilled at those words, tense. Two years ago? He didn't look at me as he spoke. Two years ago, I'd started college just after my dad died. I would have recognized this boy if I'd seen him back then. And he knew what year I was in...

"But I'd seen you before then."

I stared at the corded muscles of his forearm below his black shirt, hand on the wheel, staring straight ahead. I waited for him to finish.

"At the funeral home. When your dad died," he admitted.

"What?" I shook my head. "You knew my father?"

"My parents own the funeral home. I...I happened to be there. I was there a lot." The way he said it, it sounded like a confession. "My parents were gone more than they were around. I hung out at Maren's."

The funeral home.

I furrowed my brow. "Why? Why hang out...there?"

He pulled into a gated apartment complex, only nodding at the guard on duty, who opened up the security lever for us.

"My sister." He swallowed, and I watched his throat bob up and down. He reversed into a spot in front of a brick apartment building, stretching high in the sky. I knew of this place. It was expensive as hell. I'd looked into it before deciding on the dorm. As a joke, more than anything. There was no way I could have afforded this place, even with Holland as a roommate. Hell, even with six people as roommates.

Dante put the car in park, pressed the button to turn it off. The dashboard lights cut out.

"She killed herself. About a year before your dad died. She always liked hanging out at Maren's. She was into weird shit. Kind of like you." His tone was hard to read, almost emotionless.

I wanted to reach out to touch him. To comfort him. But I didn't. I didn't move, because he was still talking.

"And then you..." He laughed, but it was dry. Humorless. "I couldn't take my eyes off of you in art class. I knew your name already, had seen the articles in the paper. Skydiving, haunted houses..." He shook his head, staring straight ahead, arm still propped up on the steering wheel. "I saw your paintings. They were so...dark. But you didn't go out anymore. Do those things they said you did. I never spoke to you. The way you kept your head down, you never even once looked at me."

My chest felt tight. It was hard to breathe. He'd known me, for two years?

"This Halloween, though...I'd been watching you in sports psych. I wondered what your plans were. I wanted you to know I saw you, but I wanted my friends to know not to fuck with you, in case you went out. So...I fucked with you first." Finally, he looked at me. We were quiet for a minute before he spoke again. "I'm sorry," he said, and it sounded almost sincere. "I'll buy you a new pencil."

I couldn't stop the smile stretching across my face.

His own lips curved upward, just a little. "I followed you and your friend. I knew people were fucking around in that house and I couldn't stand the thought of anyone else..." He clenched his fist around the steering wheel. "Of anyone else touching you," he continued, voice hoarse. "I promised myself I would stay away from you. But when you came in with your friend, and I knew what was going on upstairs...I couldn't stay away. I wanted you to be with me. Away from anyone else's dirty little hands."

I didn't say a word. I couldn't even hear myself breathing, although I could hear my heart slamming in my chest. But I undid my seat belt with shaking fingers, then I crawled over the console between us, reached for the button to recline his seat, and when it went as far as it could, I straddled him, knees on either side of his hips.

He brought his hands up to my arms, and the smile was gone from his face.

I undid the hoodie tied around my waist and tossed it into the passenger seat.

He cupped my face in his hands. They were so warm, my skin electric where his touched mine. I bent down, my hair hanging around us. I hovered my lips over his, not quite touching him.

He trailed his hands down around my shoulders, over my sides, coming to rest at my hips.

"I don't want to do this with you in my car," he said, frowning.

I pressed my lips just above his.

"Is that so?" I whispered, feeling him harden all over again beneath me.

He didn't laugh.

"Aria…"

"You've watched me for two years." I brush my lips against his skin as I spoke.

He nodded, eyes on mine in the dark of his car, beneath my hair. "Two years," he agreed.

"How often have you imagined this?"

He slid his hands around to my backside, grabbing me. "Every single fucking day." He tilted his head back, his mouth on mine. But he didn't kiss me. "Do you like it? That I was watching you?"

I grinded my hips against him, a moan escaping my lips as I did. I could hear him breathing, feel his every breath against my mouth.

"Did you like it?" I teased. "That everyone was watching me in that house?"

He caught my lip between his teeth, snarling as he bit down. Then he let go, eyes narrowed into hazel slits as he gazed up at me. "People have always been watching you, Aria Rosen." He snaked his hands around my wrist, planted on either side of his arms. "But you... You've always been mine."

* * * *

His apartment was his alone. He told me as much, showed me his bedroom, the living room, bathroom. All that marble and leather and luxury. Then, without warning, he pushed me against the wall of his bedroom, across from his bed, one hand on my chest and the other in my hair.

"Do you want me to share you?" he asked, his voice a growl.

I barely made it up the stairs to his unit without jumping on him. The ache between my thighs had grown steadily more uncomfortable since I'd learned he'd been watching me all this time. It should have scared me. It should have sent me running.

But then I was here, under his hands, and I didn't want to be anywhere else.

I shook my head, and he tightened his fingers in my hair, my neck arching back with the movement back as he towered over me.

"That's not an answer."

I swallowed, enjoying this game. "No."

He smiled, then he turned me around, pulled me into him and walked backward, until we sat on the edge of his bed, me in his lap.

"Stand up."

I did, and he reached around, unbuttoning my jeans, pulling them down my thighs until they hit the floor and I stepped out of them. He yanked me back into his lap, hand gliding up my inner thigh, until it came to rest at the crease, right where my underwear started.

"Do you want this?" he teased in my ear.

"Dante," I whispered, "stop…"

"I never want to hear another man's name on your lips, ever again."

I threw my head back against his shoulder, arching into the hand on my thigh.

He laughed in my ear and pulled his hand away.

"Dante," I said again, making his name a moan.

"Say please, baby girl."

"Please," I begged.

He slid his fingers under the cotton of my underwear, glided up and down my slit, teasing me.

"Who are you wet for?" he asked, his voice low. He had one arm wrapped around my waist. As if I wanted to move. As if I wanted to be anywhere else but here. "For my friends? For yours?"

I shook my head. "For you," I breathed.

He pinched my clit and I squirmed in his arms, hovering over his lap, trying to get his fingers lower.

He laughed, squeezing me tighter so I couldn't move. "You're so ready, baby girl." He slid his fingers down my opening, and he pushed one inside of me. "Fuck, Aria." He added another finger and I moaned, neck arched. "You're so fucking tight." He pumped his fingers in and out of me and I grinded my hips against him.

"What do you want now?" he asked me, stilling his fingers inside of me.

I tried to move against him, to grind against his hand, but he held me still, planting a kiss to the back of my neck.

"Tell me what you want," he murmured.

"You." I twisted around to see him, to see his hazel eyes watching me in the darkness of his bedroom. "I want you."

He spread his fingers inside me, and I tried to stifle a moan. "Do you?" he asked, pulling his fingers out, running his hand along my slit. He brought his hand up, over my stomach, my tank top, up my throat, to my lips.

But when I opened my mouth, he shook his head, yanked his fingers away and put them in his mouth.

He groaned with the taste of me on his tongue, then pulled my head forward, his fingers between our mouths as he kissed me, and I licked him, tasting me.

"You taste so good," he said, his words hoarse. "Don't you, baby girl?"

I nodded, my tongue meeting his.

He moved his hand, dropping it down to my throat. "Tell me again. What you want."

My pussy throbbed, and I ground against his leg. "You," I said again.

"Just me?" he asked, stilling my hips.

I nodded, bit my lip.

"Say it," he commanded in my ear. "Say you want me. And just me."

"I only want you."

"You don't want anyone else to fuck you, Aria?"

I shook my head. "No. I'm yours."

He groaned, and stood, taking me with him, then he laid me on his bed. I watched as he shucked off his shirt, let it fall to the floor. I took in his long, lean torso, a scar along his abdomen. Then he unbuttoned his pants, slid those off, along with his boxers. I saw, with wide eyes, the length of him. The thickness of him.

"Take off your shirt," he said.

I did as he asked, tossing it from the bed. My arms crossed over my chest, covering myself from him on instinct.

He knelt on the bed, then lowered himself over me, holding himself up on his elbows.

"I want to see all of you."

I bit my lip, but after a moment, I uncrossed my arms. He held my wrists in one hand, pinned them over my head, and his gaze snaked up and down the length of my body.

"You're beautiful," he whispered, like he meant it. "You're so fucking perfect."

He let go of my wrists, but I didn't move my hands. He trailed his finger over my body, then clamped down on my thigh, spreading it, giving him access to drink in the sight of me beneath him.

Then he met my eyes again, and slowly, he lowered himself onto me, into me.

I gasped with his entrance, and he adjusted his hips, angling himself deeper.

"Jesus Christ," he muttered, eyes on my mouth. "You're so fucking tight."

We fit perfectly together.

He was slow at first, letting me get used to the feel of him. But then he moved faster, and his hand cupped my breasts, his fingers tugged at my nipples. I arched into him, my own hands still above my head.

His mouth replaced his hand, and he pulled my nipple between his teeth, but his eyes stayed glued to mine.

He picked up the pace, slamming into me with each stroke and our breath came in quickening gasps.

"Do you want me to come inside of you?" he asked me, hand in my hair.

I nodded. I was on birth control. But he...he would be the first to finish in me.

He must have seen something in my gaze because he slowed, bringing his hand back to my throat. He tightened his fingers. "Tell me," he said.

I smirked up at him, bucked my hips against him. "No."

He moved his fingers up my neck, back into my hair, until he twined it around his fist, yanking. It felt good, the pain.

He stopped moving inside me and I moaned, trying to grind on him.

"Do you let everyone come inside of you?" he asked me.

I moved my hands, dug them into his back, and his eyes flashed. He liked it.

"You'd be the first," I told him.

Then he groaned, buried his head in my neck, and pumped hard into me, once, twice, and his body shuddered against mine.

I felt his release, and I wrapped my legs around his back, pressing him deeper into me.

He eased himself out of me, lying at an angle, and his hand moved down to my clit, rubbing me, slow at first, then faster and faster.

He slipped two fingers into me, where he had just been, and his thumb kept up the circles against my nub. His mouth found my nipple, his tongue flicking against it.

I arched into his fingers and cried out his name.

He smiled against me, taking my nipple between his teeth again. He didn't move his hand from between my legs until the vibrations that ran through me stilled.

Then he rolled over, taking me in his arms, and we lay like that against one another for a long, long time.

Chapter Six

"Holland is going to kill me." It was the first thing I said when I opened my eyes and saw the hint of sunlight peeking around Dante's blackout curtains.

He pulled me into his side, under the crisp white sheets, pressed a kiss to the top of my head.

"I thought I told you I don't want to hear another man's name on your lips ever again," he murmured, turning on his side to face me.

I turned too, staring into his eyes. They were soft with sleep, and he was absolutely beautiful.

Last night, we had stayed up far too late exploring each other far too many times.

"Where did you take Holland, anyway?" I asked. I'd left my phone at the dorm, thinking I wouldn't need it if Holland and I were just going on a quick jaunt to a haunted house.

Needless to say...I'd gotten sidetracked. Or kidnapped by Dante, either one worked.

Dante put his finger to my lips, eyes narrowed at me. "Back to his dorm," he answered me anyway. "I made sure he knew you were in good hands. Or, rather...a friend did."

"Your friends don't seem...trustworthy." I said the words around his finger.

He trailed it down my chin, over my neck. "Weston is," he said, smiling at me. "The only one, really."

"Holland's still going to kill me."

Dante shook his head. "If anyone even tries to lay a hand on you," he said, eyes still on mine, "I'll kill them."

For some reason, I thought he might mean it.

"You broke my pencil," I accused him, lacing my fingers through his. "You bullied me at Cups too."

He frowned. "I wanted everyone to know you were mine."

"So, you were a dick to me?"

His eyes flashed, and he pulled me a little closer, so our legs tangled together beneath the sheets.

"I'm sorry," he said. "I'm, generally speaking, a bit of a dick. But you're mine now, Aria. And no one is going to be a dick to you ever again."

* * * *

Holland was, surprisingly, not very angry.

He opened the door to his dorm room. Dante was at my back, and Holland looked between us, taking in my bedhead and Dante's sleepy eyes.

"Look, Holland, I'm so sorry about last night but — "

"Um." Holland glanced behind him, and I realized, for the first time, he didn't have a shirt on. He didn't open the door any wider either. "Look, Aria, I really do want to hear all about your night with Mr. Basketball" — his eyes found Dante's, then met mine again—"but I've got company."

I stepped away from the door, shocked. My brow furrowed. "You...you do?" Holland hadn't dated anyone in far too long.

Holland nodded. I noticed his hair was messy too, blond curls tousled about.

"Oh. Okay." I shook my head, in shock. Halloween had turned out a bit strange for both of us, it seemed. "Um, okay. I'll talk to you later then."

I turned to go, but Dante hadn't moved.

He looked to Holland. "Tell Weston I said hello." Then he took my arm, and we made our way down the steps leading from Holland's dorm.

"What the fuck?" I whispered as we came out into the parking lot. We had walked here, and we kept on the sidewalk as we walked, Dante's arm slung around my shoulders.

Dante winked at me, then shrugged. "Weston's gay. Looks like they hit it off."

"Like we did?" I asked with a smile.

"We did more than hit it off, Aria," he said to me, spinning me around in the middle of the sidewalk to face him. "I've been waiting for you for a long, long time."

"Why did you never try before?" I asked, relishing in the feel of his hands on either side of my hips.

"I didn't think you liked me."

I laughed. "Jock, hot, rich as fuck?" I shrugged, putting my arms around his neck. "What's not to like? And besides"—I licked my lips—"your name is Dante. Definitely ranks in the top three hottest names I've ever heard."

He fought back a smile, pressed his knuckles to his mouth. "I fucking love it when you say my name."

* * * *

We showered together for the first time. Dante stared at me a lot, but, shockingly, didn't touch me. The shower had three heads, one in the center that was bigger than the other two on each side. He stayed against one side, facing me.

We'd spent the day walking around Fall's Creek, grabbing coffee at Cups — no asshole jocks in there, save for the one by my side — and we'd even ventured out to the graveyard. With Dante by my side, it hadn't felt so…terrifying.

I watched him from my side of the shower, resisted the urge to cover myself with my arms. He'd already seen all of me, but even still, being around him made me…nervous. He didn't scare me, not exactly, but his presence was disquieting.

The water beat down against his back, running over the muscles of his shoulders, his triceps, down his veiny forearms.

I soaped up quickly, rinsed off and shampooed my hair. Surprising me, I saw he had conditioner. It wasn't my first sleepover with a boy, but most of them seemed to skip conditioner, or used some atrocious two-in-one thing.

The conditioner smelled like strawberries — another pleasant surprise. I'd assumed it would be something off-putting and manly, like tire grease or whatever name marketers were coming up with for men's products these days. Then again, this was Dante. He was full of surprises. Most of them pleasant. Some of them…not.

I squirted an ample amount of it in my palm, carefully ran my fingers through my hair. I really needed a comb, and I felt a pang of something like regret when I saw some of the pink in my hair swirl down the drain. Pastel colors didn't last long, and I really should have just skipped washing my hair, but under Dante's unwavering gaze, I needed *something* to do with my hands.

He watched me carefully, then sighed, running his hand through his own dark hair. "Do you want me to help you?" he offered when my fingers got stuck in a knot. Bleached hair tended to get a little tangled.

I froze, my fingers halfway through the length of my hair.

He arched a brow, the water dropping off his cheekbones, down his jaw. Over his abs, right past his cock, still impressive even though it was only semi-hard.

God, he was perfect.

The thought made me blush and I brought my eyes back up to his to see him smirking at me.

"Y-yes," I managed to say.

"Turn around."

"Have you ever done this before?"

He didn't answer for a minute after he picked up the conditioner from the alcove in the tiled shower wall. He squirted it in his hand, put the bottle back, and then his fingers made quick work of one section of my hair.

He didn't need to answer me, the way he was so gentle and moving quickly through each strand. He'd clearly done it before. But he spoke anyway.

"Yes," he said, "I used to do my sister's hair."

I sucked in a breath. I hadn't asked about his sister. Hadn't wanted to talk about anything he wasn't comfortable discussing. I had no idea how old she had been, what she had done when she hadn't been hanging around the funeral home her parents owned.

"Yeah," he continued, as if to himself. He huffed a laugh. "She was five years younger than me." His voice grew softer and my chest tightened as his words. His memories. "I helped out with her a lot. And what do you know, she used to dye her hair funky colors too. My mom flipped out every time." He laughed, but it was quiet. Distant.

He moved his hands to another section of my hair. He was so gentle, with featherlight touches, it was almost hard to believe this was the same man who had put his hands on my throat just last night. And it was strange, the way the feel of his fingers in my hair made it a little hard to breathe, even though we'd done much, much worse.

This felt like…being taken care of.

I stayed quiet, letting him reminisce, enjoying the feel of his hands in my hair. But I wanted more. It was a little unnerving, knowing he had watched me for so long and up until yesterday, I hadn't even known he had existed.

"What's the worst thing you've ever done?" I asked suddenly, the sound of the water lulling me into a placid calm, the steam of the shower enveloping us, making it seem as if we were the only two people in the world. We were in a little bubble in this glass shower, and no one could touch us. No one could break us.

And in here, I wanted his secrets. I wanted to know more. See beyond the asshole front he put up. He'd given me a glimpse, talking about his sister, but it wasn't enough.

His fingers stilled, but only for a moment. "It's not a good post-sex conversation," he said, and I couldn't really decipher his tone. I didn't know if he was still thinking about his sister and I had interrupted his memories, or if he just really didn't want to have this conversation right now.

I twisted my hands together under the warm water. "I want to hear it anyway."

He ran his fingers through my hair. No more knots. "No, you really don't, Aria."

Then he turned the showerheads off.

I didn't want to think about how stupid I was, to think he'd tell me something so personal. I reached for the shower door first, the metal bar along the inside of the glass door, but he reached too, his chest at my back.

His fingers curled around mine.

"Aren't you going to thank me?" he asked, his breath hitting my neck.

"T-thank you," I managed to say. I made to push the door open. He gripped my hand tighter, not letting me put leverage against the door.

"Aria.

"Dante?"

"What's the worst thing *you've* ever done?"

My mouth fell open, my breath catching in my throat. I suddenly wanted to be alone. I wanted to run out of this shower, fling my clothes back on, and leave his apartment. Get back to my own. My corner of the world with Holland. A corner that definitely did not have room for jocks that were out of my league.

I wanted to escape.

"Answer me, Aria." His tone wasn't angry, but it was harder, clipped. He pressed his hand possessively against mine.

But he didn't get to call the shots on everything.

I spun around, slipping against his body, yanking my hand from his. I looked up at him, my eyes narrowed. "No. *You* answer *me*."

His brows flicked up in surprise, but I saw a hint of a smile on his face. "Aria," he said, his tone laced with warning, "that's not really how things work between us —"

I slapped his chest, left my palm against his wet, warm body. "Please," I begged him, making my voice soft, "you know a lot about me. I don't know anything about you."

He just stared at me.

I trailed my hand down his chest, over his abs. "Come on, Dante," I pleaded. "Give me something."

He rolled his eyes, tipping his head up, but I knew I'd won. I was sure there'd be more battles to come with someone as arrogant and domineering as he was, but this was a victory I didn't take lightly.

"You wanna discuss this in the shower?" he asked, dipping his chin to lock eyes with me again, his gaze trailing over my body. "Because if so, I might get distracted. It was hard enough to keep my fingers only in your hair."

I laughed, turning away from him. "We can get out," I agreed, "and then you're talking."

* * * *

I sat pressed against the pillows of his bed, my knees tucked into my chest. I wore one of his T-shirts and a pair of loose-fitting boxers, the covers pulled up over my legs. He was beside me, one arm draped around my body as he scrolled through the movies available for us to watch on the flat-screen TV mounted across from his bed.

He'd helped me towel dry my hair — apparently, I couldn't be trusted to groom myself alone — and we'd manage to make it into bed without more than a few inappropriate grabs.

"The worst thing I ever did," he said, still looking at the TV, "was ignore my gut."

I frowned, my body stiff as I waited for him to keep talking. Obviously, he was referring to something specific. But what, I didn't know.

He blew out a breath, still scrolling, but I could tell he wasn't really seeing anything on the screen. "Dacia, my sister...she had been struggling for a few...years. Mom and Dad weren't home a lot. I took care of her more than they did, although they had a nanny and I guess they figured that was a fine substitute for any actual parenting." He grimaced, finally gave up the pretense of scrolling and dropped the remote on the bed.

His arm tightened around me, but he still didn't look at me.

"Anyway" — he sighed — "it didn't bother me, the way they weren't around. Not like it bothered her. I had sports and my friends, but she..." He twisted his head to look at me, a faint smile on his lips. "She was like you, and she didn't have those...distractions."

I reached over, under the covers and placed my hand against his knee, squeezing him. He leaned back against the pillows, dragging me with him, my head against his chest. He tightened his grip on me.

"She started to kind of...withdraw. I let it go, just dismissed it as normal adolescent angst." He laughed to himself. "Girl stuff that I didn't have time for." He turned on his side and I did too, to face him. He linked his fingers in mine, between us on the bed, his hazel eyes on mine.

"I knew better. But I let it go. And then..." He trailed off, looking down at our entwined fingers. "She was gone." His voice was hoarse on those last words, and I watched him swallow.

I didn't know what to say, but he didn't seem to need me to say anything at all. I just watched him, letting the silence envelope us, giving us comfort. I wondered what Dacia had been like. I wondered what his parents were like.

Wondered how his sister's death affected them.

After a moment, he looked up at me again and smiled. "Didn't think such a dick had it in him to have a heart, did you?"

I rolled my eyes, squeezed his fingers as his gaze softened. "I knew there was more to you than met the eye, Dante Llera."

"How's that? I broke your stupid pencil—"

I shot him a glare.

"Sorry," he amended, bringing my fingers up to kiss them, "I broke your very professional and slightly nerdy mechanical pencil, and threatened to throw hot coffee on you at Cups." He shrugged. "You had every right to think I was just a heartless asshole."

"Oh, I *still* think that." I slid closer to him, so our legs were touching under the covers. "But you happen to be kind of sweet when you want to be, and your sister sounds like a girl I would've really liked." I squeezed his fingers again. "For her sake, I think it's only fair I give you a shot."

He let go of my hand, wrapped his arm around my back and pulled me in close. He shifted on the bed and moved me with him, so I was lying on my back and he was propped up on one elbow, looking down at me.

"Now it's your turn, baby girl," he said, trailing his finger down my jaw. "What's the worst thing you've ever done?"

"Oh, that's easy," I said, adopting a very serious tone. "The worst thing *I've* ever done is let a hot asshole corner me in an abandoned house, drag me back to his apartment and —"

He clamped his hand over my mouth, silencing my words. He leaned down close, and a chill slid down my spine as I felt his breath caress my ear. "We were talking about the *worst* thing you ever did, baby girl, not the *best.*"

I laughed behind his hand. "That is the worst!" I protested, my words muffled.

He grazed his lips against my ear, slid his hand down from my mouth, over my chin, to my throat. His fingers tightened and I sucked in a breath, the little hairs on my arms standing on end. "Is that so?" he asked me, pulling back, his eyes on mine.

I nodded, biting my lip.

His eyes flicked to my mouth, his hand trailing down over my breast, circling my hard nipple through my shirt.

"I don't think so, Aria," he whispered, going lower. He skimmed over my low belly, then his hand slipped inside the boxers of his I was wearing. He circled his fingers between my thighs, barely touching me, and I whimpered, lifting my hips to meet his hand.

He laughed, pressed a kiss to the side of my neck. I angled my head, giving him better access. He ran his tongue down my throat, his fingers on the inside of my thighs.

"Dante," I murmured, bucking my hips more. Warmth spooled in my belly, and I wanted his fingers *inside* me.

"Yes, baby girl?" he asked, his breath hot against my throat. But he still didn't touch me where I wanted him to—instead, he kept playing against my inner thighs, featherlight strokes that did nothing but tease.

"Stop fucking around," I mumbled, my eyes closed.

He kissed my neck and laughed against my skin. "So mouthy." His voice was low, and it made my stomach knot in anticipation. "But if I'm the worst thing you've ever done"—he pulled his fingers off of me—"maybe I should...stop?"

I snapped my eyes open and turned my head to glare up at him. "Don't you dare."

He smirked at me. "Or?"

"Or I'll walk out of here right now and go find your little friend." I flashed what I hoped was a devilish smile up at him. "*Scott.*"

His eyes narrowed and he clamped his hand down over my thigh.

"Or that guy we saw in the driveway—"

"Shut up."

I almost shivered at the tone of his voice, but I kept my eyes locked on his. Didn't let myself betray any more of my desire than I already had. "Or what?" I taunted him. "What're you going to do about it, *Dante*?"

He shifted his body on top of mine, all of his weight pressing me against the bed. He had his forearm against my throat. I could still breathe, but it was uncomfortable.

Uncomfortable, but with his erection pressing against my stomach, it was gratifying, too. A forewarning of what was to come.

He reached between us, shifting us hips, and then he slid the boxers down my hips. I tilted them up, helping him get them down to my knees.

He pulled off his own shorts, pushed himself up.

My eyes widened as he pressed more of his weight against my throat. He quickly shifted his position, planted his hand on the mattress, beside my head.

I gasped for air and before I could catch my breath, he positioned his cock against me and pushed into me, digging his fingers into my hips.

"*Fuck,*" he uttered, closing his eyes for a second. "Even when you're acting like a little brat, you feel so fucking good."

I wrapped my legs around his back, my arms around his chest.

He pressed his forehead to mine and slowed inside of me.

"What?" I asked, a little breathless.

He tangled his fingers through my hair, gripped the base of my skull. "You are so damn beautiful, Aria." He angled his head and snatched up my lips, moving again inside me, slower this time.

When he finally pulled away, I ran my tongue over my swollen mouth, gasping for air.

"And so damn mine."

HOT OFF
THE PRESS

Chapter One

It was such a great dream. Jax was stretched out on a sandy beach, feeling the sun warm her skin and smelling the salt on the air—just like home. She could taste mango on her lips, and there was no sound but the waves and the distant chirping of birds. Sure, their calls were a little weird, but then she hadn't been back to the island in a long time. Maybe she'd forgotten some of the details.

Slowly, Jax opened her eyes, watched her bedroom ceiling swim into focus, and realized where the noise was coming from.

"Oh, shit!"

She kicked off the covers and grabbed her phone, struggling to shut off the chirruping bleep that should have woken her thirty-five minutes ago. What in the hell had possessed her to use a new alarm app on a morning like this?

Heart pounding, Jax leaped out of bed in a flurry of swearing and panic, and almost tripped over her laundry hamper.

"God damn it!" she yelped, giving the wicker a solid kick.

Of *course* she'd oversleep today. Her interview with Paula Cox—design mogul, legendary entrepreneur and one of the biggest donors Stockard College had—was a coup for a humble student journalist, the kind of byline Jax had been working toward for her whole three years on the school's prestigious media program. Of *course* she'd find a way to screw things up, or make it harder for herself, because when didn't she?

A knock at the door sounded as Jax was halfway through stripping off her sleep cami and panties, and grabbing the day's clothes from the hanger on the front of her wardrobe.

"Um… Jax? You up?" Ava's voice came through the white-painted wood. "It's gone seven thirty and I didn't see you yet, so—"

Jax, still shimmying into her bra and trying to find a spare pair of hands to fasten her skirt, paused to wrench open the door.

"Late!" she squeaked. "*So* late! Oh, god…"

Her roommate, as put together as always, raised one perfect brow and pursed her lips. "You don't say. Oh, hon. You slept with wet hair again, didn't you?"

Jax, buttoning her shirt and shoving her feet into a polished pair of black pumps, looked up in horror.

"Why?"

Ava shook her head. "All right, all right…don't worry. We'll fix it. I've got time. I brought your papers, too, though I have no idea why you guys don't just read the apps. Like, there's old school and *old school*, you know?"

She tossed a handful of folded newspapers onto the bed before moving across the room to grab Jax's hot air brush from the dresser. Jax glanced at the headlines out of habit—something about a city council funding inquiry, and another fire in the industrial district, the sixth in five months — and gave a bitter grin.

"Right? They tell us it's so we get used to being on top of the news…learning what leads and what gets buried, since not every story shows up on a paper's app. Either that, or the media department's getting a cut of all newspaper sales on campus. Which I could believe," she added, hastily stuffing her cream cotton shirt into her skirt in an uneven tuck that made Ava wince.

"Here. Lemme get that."

Jax huffed a sigh and held her arms out to the side, letting Ava tweak her look.

They'd been rooming since freshman year, having bonded despite a bumpy start. At first, Jax had thought the design major was stuck-up and bitchy, and Ava had — she'd confessed one night, after some ill-advised peach schnapps — thought Jax was a neurotic, prissy mess who just wanted attention. Somewhere along the way, though, they'd realized how well they worked together. Like the exact opposite of that damn schnapps and cola.

"I owe you," Jax said, patting a few quick dabs of primer across her cheeks and scrambling for her lipstick as Ava positioned her in front of the mirror and addressed the frizzy tangle of her strawberry blonde waves.

"I know."

"This *never* happens! I mean — "

"I know. You've been late, like, what? Twice this semester? Or was it three times? Or maybe — "

"Stop it!" Jax groaned. "It would be today. Because of course it would. Oh, *man*… Ask me questions about Paula Cox, would you? I have to make sure I know the material."

Ava looked doubtful. "It's not exactly going to be a hard-hitting exposé, Jax. She's a big donor, and it's a college paper, so—"

"I know, I know...but it's part of my final grade. So just work with me. Please?"

Ava sighed. "All right. Hit me with some of that sweet, sweet bio, Miss Wiki. Birth, background... Go!"

Jax closed her eyes. Facts were good. She could *do* facts. "Okay. Born in seventy-three, grew up in northern California but relocated to Oregon in twenty-thirteen, after the multi-million-dollar sale of her design company, Cohan. She studied at Caltech, but there's a family connection to the Stockards who founded the college here in Dalesburg, so she established the Cox Scholarship to reconnect with—"

"Some sense of legitimacy beyond just throwing money at life?" Ava supplemented.

Jax, trying to apply her mascara without laughing, stifled a snort. "Ava! You're terrible."

"I'm just saying! You've got this, sis. It's going to be fine. This lady gets rich off of people buying her proto-hipster crap and donates a bunch of money here because there's nothing like having your name on a library to make you feel legitimized. That's all. Say nice things about her, throw out some of your sparkling prose...y'know. You got it."

"You think so?"

"*Think*?" Ava smoothed out Jax's hair, now falling in soft curves around her shoulders, and reached for the pump bottle of finishing oil on the dresser. "I *know* it. You may feel like a hot mess, hon, but you're stronger than you think, and you're good at this. You're going to be just fine. And you're going to pick up pizza on your way home. I've got the afternoon free, and I feel like movies and junk food. You'll probably be able to use that yourself after your audience with Queen Consumerism."

Jax rolled her eyes, though it did sound like a tempting plan. "What, like you never got a Cohan tote bag for your birthday, and actually *used* it?"

Ava grinned. "I have *no* idea what you're talking about. Like I'd buy into those bougie mass-market aesthetics…! Here," she added, holding up a granola bar and waggling it at Jax's reflection. "You can cram that in your face as you're running across campus and trying to make it look like a power jog."

Jax shook her head. "How is it that you're the mom friend and the sarcastic bitch friend at the same time?"

"Talent." Ava gave a saccharine smile and patted her shoulders. "You look great. You're going to kill it."

"Veggie Supreme, right?"

"Yes, please. No olives."

"Gotcha. All right, gotta run. See you later!"

* * * *

Jax rushed across campus—more or less as Ava had predicted, with a mouthful of granola and a good effort at not looking as if she were panicking—and made it to Room 130 in the Media Studies building with less than a minute to spare.

Dr. Reilly was already there, along with a couple of freshmen clutching coffee mugs and staring blearily at a morning news stream on someone's laptop. The lecturer turned as Jax slipped through the door, doing her best to make it look as though she hadn't been running down the hallway.

"Ah, Ms. North! Good morning!"

Jax turned on a sunny smile. "Morning, Dr. Reilly. How are you?"

The lecturer gave a weary smile before raising her travel mug to her lips. It was decorated with several stickers, most likely chosen by her kids. One of them showed a narwhal flanked by two smaller narwhals, with the words 'mermaid unicorn mom' underneath in curly letters.

"My youngest is teething. Sleep is a distant memory. Are you all prepped for today?"

Jax nodded. "Absolutely. Um. Is Kendra here yet? Because we should really —"

Dr. Reilly waved a hand, busy taking a gulp of her coffee. "Ah! Damn it. I should have texted you. Sorry. She's out sick — food poisoning, poor thing — so I've set you up with an alternative photographer. One of my grad students. He's late, actually. He promised me he'd be here by quarter to eight. Do you know Lucas Hargrove?"

Jax opened her mouth, but no words were brave enough to cross her lips.

"H-Hargrove?" she managed. "Seriously?"

"Come now, Ms. North." Dr. Reilly looked amused. "He's not as bad as all that. Certainly nothing like you've heard, I'm sure."

"Oh, I didn't mean —"

"Yes, you did." Dr. Reilly took a sip of her coffee, raising her eyebrows suggestively over the rim of her mug. "And nobody would blame you. I'm well aware Lucas has quite the reputation on campus, but he's perfectly capable of behaving...and he's a good photographer, when he chooses to show up."

Jax deflated. The last thing she needed to contend with today was the football-field-sized ego of a wealthy, primped asshole like Lucas Hargrove. Of course she knew his name, though she'd never seen him on campus. Everyone knew the Hargroves. The family had owned half the county's factories back in the day, and in recent years had been at the forefront of diversifying Dalesburg's dying industries into shiny new tech firms.

Their name was plastered over a bunch of buildings downtown, so it was no surprise to the student body that the youngest Hargrove was slumming his way through a small private school like Stockard, because his parents had paid just as much to get him in as they had to keep his bad behavior out of the spotlight.

"It's just…this means a lot to me," Jax said, her words hesitant. "I worked hard to prep this, and I don't want to be let down by someone who can't even show up on time. Someone who…well, *is* kind of known just for being a flake, more interested in partying and working his way through the sorority girls instead of actually doing any work, so—"

"Morning, Dr. Reilly."

Jax's stomach flipped. Because *of course*. She'd never met him in person or heard his voice before, but she knew it was him. It couldn't have been anyone else—the air of entitlement dripped from his words, though it wasn't quite enough to dispel Jax's raging embarrassment, which threatened to swallow her whole.

Dr. Reilly smiled. "Mr. Hargrove. Nice of you to join us at last, and it's only a quarter past eight. This is Ms. North, with whom you'll be working today." She moved to her desk and picked up a yellow folder. "I've got your press packet here. Now, I suggest you get a move on. Traffic's going to be a nightmare if you leave it too long, and I'm sure the illustrious Ms. Cox isn't used to being kept waiting."

Jax plastered a smile across her lips as she turned, ready to greet Rich Boy McPrivilegeface and try to find some way of apologizing for her graceless first impression.

He was lounging against the door frame, car keys in his hand and a camera bag over his shoulder, bored nonchalance etched into his features. She wasn't sure what she'd expected — some corn-fed blond frat boy, perhaps, with an idiotic grin and the attention span of a flea, or maybe some oily rich kid in a pair of overpriced shades — but neither of those things seemed to be Lucas Hargrove's style.

He was tall, with wavy dark hair curling around his face in a manner that had probably been called 'cherubic' when he was a little kid. Jax recognized his kind of look at once. A charming dimpled smile, big brown eyes that could no doubt shine with honesty, and the kind of handsomeness that got him out of trouble with as much ease as he got into it… Oh, yes, she'd met guys like him before. The resorts used to crawl with them in the summers.

He wore expensive-looking jeans and a light blue shirt, rolled up to his forearms and buttoned tight across his broad-shouldered build. He wasn't big in a way that suggested he played much sport or lived in the gym — his type didn't tend to commit to things long enough to do either of those — but no doubt he played tennis or swam or something. He certainly looked fit, and Jax reminded herself that noticing that was her well-trained observational skills and nothing more. He opened his mouth and addressed their lecturer in a voice dripping with scorn.

"I'm sure she'll be just fine. It's not like she's expecting *The New Yorker* to roll by for a chat, right?"

"Be that as it may," Dr. Reilly said, her tone sharp as she held out the folder containing their credentials, "you're representing the college, and yourselves. I know I don't have to remind you that today is important, but I will wish you luck."

"Thank you, Dr. Reilly. I'm sure—"

Jax lifted her hand, ready to take the press packet, but Lucas reached across her, plucking the folder from Dr. Reilly's hand and leaving the words shriveling on Jax's lips. She blinked up at him.

He glanced at Jax, acknowledging her presence for the first time. "So, are you ready to head out? We'll take my car."

He strode past her without a backward glance. Jax winced and looked to Dr. Reilly for some crumb of support. The professor sipped a mouthful of coffee, shrugged and gave Jax a small, hopeful smile that said *you'll be fine…probably.*

Jax sighed and headed after her new partner.

"Hey, wait a minute!"

She caught up with Lucas in the hallway, damned if she was going to run to reach him. He paused by a bulletin board papered with accommodation and seminar flyers, and glanced back at her in surprise.

"What's the matter? Not worried about being on time for your big interview?"

Jax stared. "Excuse me? You got to the room after me, and then you just sweep out of there without a word, a…a 'good morning' or—"

"Oh, I'm sorry." He smirked. "*Good morning.* Is that better?"

"That's not the p—"

"Listen, you can complain about my lack of manners in the car, I promise. Just let's get going, okay?"

Irritation bubbled under Jax's skin, but she bit her tongue and hurried after him as he strode out through the double doors and toward the parking lot. She was a little surprised that he bothered to hold the door for her. She'd been planning to apologize for what she'd said to Dr. Reilly, but now she couldn't even tell if he was mad at her, or just treated everyone he thought was below his notice this way.

A frown pinched Lucas' brow as he looked down at her.

"What did you say your name was, anyway?"

"I didn't. But it's Jax. Jax North."

"Oh. Short for Jacqueline? Why don't you just go by Jackie or something?"

Jax blinked. "Because...that isn't my name? And I happen to prefer Jax. Thanks."

He glanced at her almost as if he were confused, but the fleeting sense of interest seemed to fall away and he went back to striding ahead.

Outside, the early summer sun was bright, the sky a sharp blue that had Jax squinting even as she frowned at Lucas' back. She cursed under her breath and hurried to catch up with him. Again.

"So," he asked, without turning to look at her, "why are you taking journalism?"

"Why are you interested?" Jax countered, allowing suspicion to hang in her tone.

He laughed — a surprisingly warm sound — but didn't look back. "What? I'm not allowed to ask questions? I'm just curious."

She doubted that. It felt like a set-up, but she had little to lose. Jax shrugged, following him across the lot.

"I care about people knowing the truth. I want to make a difference in the kind of world we all live in, and I figure a good way to do that is by being part of the media that shapes our society."

"Really?" Lucas scoffed. "Nice. You got that well-rehearsed. That answer swing you past the interview panel, did it?"

She gritted her teeth. "Well, if it did, it's nice knowing I didn't need to rely on my family's checking account to get me in."

His grin widened and he chuckled to himself. "Ooh, nice. Your classism's showing, you know. Where are you from, anyway? Some plucky little mining town in one of the Dakotas?"

"I— No. Why would...? No, you know what? It doesn't matter. What exactly is your problem with me?"

"Who said I had a problem?" He turned those big brown eyes on her and—just as she'd predicted—there was that cherubic smile, all innocence and sweetness, though it was gone in a second and it never seemed to reach his eyes. "*I'm* the one who got up and got my ass in here to cover for whatshername, who's supposed to be the photographer, as a favor to Dr. Reilly. I had plans today, you know. Running around half the city after some dumb donor puff piece isn't exactly my first choice for a scintillating day, and I don't need you dragging me for something I'm doing to try and help."

Jax actually took a step backward, surprised by the strength of his sudden irritation. His brows had drawn low, but the scowl on his face didn't seem to be directed at her. Then, in the barest of moments, his lips twisted and the storm seemed to clear from his eyes.

Lucas ran a hand over his hair, sighed, and shook his head. "Sorry. I don't mean to be an asshole—"

"You could have fooled me."

"Nice. Thanks. Look, shall we just start over?" He held out his hand to her. "Hi. My name's Lucas. I'm going to be your photographer today."

Jax looked at him, doubt narrowing her eyes. The sunshine outlined his broad shoulders in a corona of gold and picked at the chestnut tones in his dark hair. She got the feeling that starting over and switching on the charm was something that worked for him every single time but, if she wanted to get through today, there was no sense in being churlish.

She slipped her hand into his broad, large palm, and his warm fingers curled gently around hers. That was a surprise. She'd have figured him for a bone-crushing, dominance-asserting, handshake kind of guy.

"Jax North," she said. "Thanks for stepping in at the last minute."

Lucas inclined his head. "Sure. All right, this is me. Let's go."

He nodded to a shiny silver Nissan Leaf at the corner of the lot and pulled out his keys.

Jax quirked an eyebrow. "What, no Maserati?"

He shot her a look somewhere between amusement and annoyance. "No, but Mother says she's planning on buying me a Tesla Model S when I'm done with school."

"Seriously?"

The word slipped out, drenched in scorn, before Jax could stop it, but she had the grace to feel at least a little embarrassed. The corner of Lucas' lips curved upward in a sarcastic smirk.

"No. But there you go again with your prejudice."

"Prejudice?" Jax laughed as she opened the passenger-side door and slipped into the pristine interior. He was definitely the 'clean car, dirty mind' type, she decided. The Leaf looked as if he'd just driven it off the lot. "I wouldn't call it that. Anyway, surely you can't blame me. You *are* one of *those* Hargroves, right?"

He shrugged and adjusted the rearview mirror before setting his hands at ten and two on the wheel. She couldn't help but be amused at the precision of the gesture—he didn't seem the type to be such a stickler.

"Yeah, sure. Whatever that means. If you're going to keep complaining about it, though, this is going to be a really long day."

"I'm just curious," Jax said, keeping her voice breezy and trying to avoid the fact that he did have a point. "Why Stockard? Why a journalism course? Dr. Reilly says you're a grad student."

Lucas groaned. "Oh, come on… I thought I was done with going around the room and saying my name and my major after the end of freshman year. It took long enough. All right, all right…you got me. All I ever wanted was to be a news anchor. I guess it's the snazzy neckties, the tooth bleach and the hours in the makeup chair."

Jax snorted, despite herself. "Not fair. I gave you a good answer. And you *did* ask me the same thing."

He shrugged as he started the car. The radio clicked onto a station that was apparently hosting a discussion on water rights and pipeline disputes. Lucas turned it off and focused on backing out of his space.

"All right, Amy Goodman! Jeez. Same as you, then. I think the truth's important. And I figured taking a master's in media gives me a deeper understanding of the industry than I'd get otherwise, plus it stops my dad asking me when I'm going to be a good boy and go take up a CMO post on his new pet project, or whatever else he wants me to do at the time. Happy?"

It disconcerted her to realize that she couldn't tell if he was kidding or not. He'd said it with another smirk, that slick kind of self-satisfied smile Jax was all too used to seeing on men like him, but this time there was more warmth in his eyes. She saw it when he glanced into the rearview mirror and—with the sunlight slanting across his killer cheekbones—she found his reflection's gaze resting on her for a second before he looked away.

Jax turned her head, watching the world from the car window, and focused on mentally rehearsing her interview questions.

Chapter Two

They made it to Crane Plaza — the business park in the center of town, bristling with glass-fronted, solar-panel-covered office buildings and a clutch of eco-build boutiques and bistros — in good time, missing the rush-hour traffic thanks to Lucas' shortcut skills.

"Can't take all the credit," he said, easing the Leaf into a vacant space. "My father used to have an office down here. I'd go hang out there with him sometimes after school, if he had stuff to do after he'd picked me up from swim class."

"That sounds...lonely," Jax admitted.

Lucas shot her a withering look as he pulled the keys from the ignition. "Not really. I got to see a lot of cool stuff. I liked the peace and quiet, too. And no, I didn't have a driver."

Jax's eyebrows rose. "I didn't—"

"You were thinking it. I could hear the tiny wheels turning in that judgy little head of yours. All right, let's go. Oh. One second."

Without warning, he leaned over and reached toward her face, his expression serious and intense. Jax stiffened, her breath catching. She could smell a trace of something spicy—a sandalwood soap, perhaps?—on his skin, and his touch was warm, assured. Far *too* goddamn assured, she reminded herself.

Lucas bit his lip and hooked his finger into her hair, tucking it behind her ear before he swept his hand across her bangs. Jax, too stunned to do anything but let it happen, watched in amazement as he frowned, studying her.

"There," he said, satisfied. "Fixed it."

"You 'fixed' it?" she echoed incredulously. "*Excuse me?*"

"Your bangs were messed up, and your hair looks much better that way. Shows off your jaw line. Way sharper. More...professional," he added, with a touch of that sarcastic smirk at his lips. "I like your earrings, though."

Before she could help herself, Jax reached up to touch the gold stud in her ear which he had exposed. It was shaped like a leaping dolphin. She'd forgotten she was even wearing them, but the earrings were a little reminder of home, something that grounded her in a moment that had seemed to send the world spinning into confusion.

"I bet you were one of those girls who always wanted to swim with dolphins, weren't you?" Lucas chuckled to himself as he got out of the car. "Ever go to Miami?"

Jax willed her legs to work as she stepped out onto the curb, the press packet clutched to her chest and the questions she'd prepped bouncing around her head like hailstones.

"No," she said, trying to focus. "And also no, I didn't. They're cool, but messing with them is generally pretty confusing and stressful for the pods. Tourists get excited about it, but we try to just let the dolphins do their thing, y'know?"

"Wh—"

"Let's go," Jax said, ignoring his confusion, her voice bright and crisp.

She walked past him toward the shiny glass doors of the entrance, her heels clicking on the pavement, and it was a boost to her equilibrium *and* her ego to see that— for the first time today—Lucas Hargrove was actually speechless.

Of course, that joy didn't last long.

As soon as they were inside the building that housed the offices of Cox Consulting, Lucas was overtaking her again, striding up to the front desk in his usual cocky manner.

The receptionist was taking a call, so they hung back and waited a little. Jax looked up at the cavernous foyer space, with its arched ceiling and white walls dotted with muted abstract canvases. The floor was shinier than her kitchen worktops.

"So, where did you grow up that had dolphins?" Lucas asked.

Jax hadn't realized he was standing so close behind her, and his breath stirred the hair on the back of her neck, his voice a hushed rumble that was surprisingly soft and intimate. She blinked, focusing on a painting hanging on the wall opposite them, her gaze following its sinuous blue-and-green spirals. The scent of him— that rich, spicy, clean fragrance—tugged at her senses, and she absolutely, positively refused to acknowledge the fact that it made her nipples tighten.

"Saint Lucia," she said, trying to keep her voice light and casual. "My grandparents ran a small hotel on the island. I was born in Washington, lived near Seattle when

I was little, and then we moved out to the island when I was about nine. I came back here full-time to study."

It was a decidedly flat way of conveying what had been some of the strangest, best, most complicated times in her life to date, but Jax had no real desire to dump her whole life story on Lucas Hargrove. He'd no doubt have some shit to say about it, anyway.

He was quiet for now, though. Perhaps too quiet. She risked a glance up at him, taking in the furrowed brow and thoughtful look in his dark eyes.

"What?"

He was looking at her without shame, not even trying to hide his careful study of her face, as if he was analyzing her like some fascinating lab specimen. Jax held his gaze, unwilling to give him the satisfaction of looking away, no matter how exposed she felt. The heat of a blush threatened to crest her neck, and she willed it down. Who the hell did this guy think he was, anyway?

Lucas' full lips quirked upward, and he raised an eyebrow.

"Nothing. You're just...not what I expected of someone who grew up in the Caribbean. You don't seem like the, uh, type."

"Type?" Jax echoed acidly. "And what *type* is that, exactly? Box braids and beach parties?"

"No."

He seemed a little put out, though there was no real heat in his tone. He watched her, curiosity in his eyes, and Jax found herself meeting his gaze, jutting out her chin as if daring him to say something snarky. She'd heard plenty of those jokes since coming back.

Lucas just looked at her. There was no apology in his face.

Jax huffed, unsure why his attitude bothered her so much.

"People usually have something to say," she admitted. "Y'know. They assume I'm a party girl, like there's nothing else to the islands except fruity drinks and beaches. It's not like that. Sure, it's beautiful, and it's wonderful to go hang out on the beach… I miss that. But, I mean, *nothing* is that simple, right? Everywhere has its own identity, its problems and the things that make it special."

"Yeah." Lucas' voice was warm and smooth, but with an unmistakable tang of sarcasm. "It's almost as if you shouldn't judge people based on your preconceptions, isn't it? Or is that the kind of thing an overprivileged rich guy would say? You know, the kind more used to partying and working his way through the sorority girls instead of doing any actual work?"

Jax winced. She'd known he'd heard that, but she hadn't expected to feel so bad about it. "Look, I'm sorry. I shouldn't have—"

Her apology was cut off as the receptionist finished her call, and Lucas asked for their arrival to be phoned through. He seemed to take charge without even thinking about it, and Jax—too embarrassed to argue—followed him dumbly toward the elevator, trying to concentrate on the job ahead instead of the gnawing knot of humiliation nestled in her stomach. How *dare* he make her feel guilty for being right about him? After all, what the hell else was Lucas Hargrove, aside from a spoiled rich kid and a royal pain in her ass?

* * * *

The office was large, plush and full of awards and tasteful mementoes—just the kind of thing Jax had expected from a woman who'd built a successful career and was reaping its rewards in consultancy. She just wished she'd expected the reaction that came when Lucas walked into the room, too.

"Paula! Long time." He smiled and held out one long, broad hand. "It's so nice to see you."

Jax tried not to stare. Of *course* they knew each other. Why wouldn't they? Why wouldn't there be just one more reason he could look down at her, one more thing he hadn't bothered to tell her? She gritted her teeth and tried to smile through the urge to kick Lucas right in the ass.

"Lucas? Oh my goodness! What a wonderful surprise."

Paula Cox smiled as she shook his hand and leaned in to kiss his cheek. She was tall, elegant and pristine in a dark navy skirt suit. *Must be tough to close an account at three and be ready for cocktails at the country club by four*, Jax thought bitterly.

So much for her big interview and her important byline. In a second, she'd gone from the person in charge of the interview to Lucas' bag carrier. *Just great.*

"How is your mother? I haven't seen her in ages."

"She's good. Still working on that fundraiser thing for the symphony. You know how she is about her causes," Lucas added, grimacing. "Not that it isn't important, of course…"

Paula grinned with the air of a woman indulging a mischievous child.

"Be careful, kid. Your mom and I both spent years on that youth orchestra committee."

Lucas flashed his best charming, boyish grin, his dark eyes full of mischief. "Oh, I know. I just *love* the arts!" He turned to Jax. "Anyway, shall we get started?"

Irritation burned on the back of Jax's tongue. She couldn't believe this was happening. Everything she'd worked for, everything she'd planned, and he made her feel like an imposter, a fool. The audacity he had, to just march into her day and turn everything upside down…and she couldn't say a damn thing about it without seeming crazy, as if she was the one with the problem.

Jax's fingers fumbled a little as she took out her notes, recorder and the press packet Dr. Reilly had given them – like they needed credentials, with *him* here – and tried to focus on the task in hand. She dredged up every bit of enthusiasm she could manage and smiled her best professional smile.

"Well, um, let me start by saying thank you for meeting with us, Ms. Cox. I wanted to ask you in particular about how you got your start with your first company, Cohan, and where the idea to form what could be called the first online lifestyle brand came from…"

The interview should have gone well. In theory, it did.

Paula Cox was a gracious host. She offered them seats in her plush, comfortable chairs and coffee courtesy of her PA, and everything was just as it should have been…except that it wasn't, because Jax couldn't help herself snatching looks at the smug, arrogant asshole she was stuck with, who'd thrown her so badly off her game and who just wouldn't stop adding to her woes.

They talked about all the right things, hit all the right notes a piece for a college paper should hit – entrepreneurial spirit, the zeitgeist that Paula Cox had tapped into in order to build her brand, and of course the importance of those big educational donations.

Jax hated to admit it, but Lucas had been right – there was nothing ground-breaking here. Still, she admired the woman and the career she'd built for herself, and the half-hour they spent in her company was pretty inspiring. At least, it would have been, if it hadn't felt so much like Jax was sitting in on a lunch date with someone else's friend.

Paula kept glancing over to Lucas, sometimes talking to him more than Jax, and, when it came to him taking the pictures, they might as well have been a Hargrove family Christmas card shoot.

Jax kept her smile in place and her feelings under control. He was right—this was a puff piece, a little donor flattery that Dr. Reilly was deploying to keep her bosses happy. How dumb had Jax been not to see it? She felt stupid, childish…useless. Worst of all, every time she shot a look at Lucas—sitting there smiling, looking so at home in this lush, professional setting—he made her feel a little bit angrier, the heat of irritation and something not unlike jealousy itching beneath her skin.

* * * *

The whole thing was over fast, which was a blessing. Jax managed to hold herself together as she thanked Paula Cox, said goodbye, and made it out to the elevator.

She glared at Lucas as he joined her in the elevator and, as the doors swished closed behind him, Jax's anger spilled out.

"What in the hell was that?"

Lucas' eyebrows shot up. "What's the matter with you?" he demanded. "I thought you were excited for your big scoop."

Jax stared at him in disbelief. "Really? You've got no idea?"

"No. I'm not a goddamn mind reader. So why don't you enlighten me?"

"That was supposed to be *my* break! *My* interview! Instead, you just waltzed in there and had tea with your goddamn Auntie Paula and left me sitting there like an idiot. Fuck you, Lucas. Fuck your...your stupid little world, and your stupid thick head!"

Jax's mouth snapped shut, her pulse pounding. She hadn't meant to respond with such venom or aggression, and the words echoed in her head, sounding so stupid and malformed.

Lucas stared at her, aghast, then an odd look of hurt realization filtered across his eyes. "Wait...you think I did that to humiliate you?"

"Didn't you?"

"No! Why the hell would I do that?"

"I don't know!" Jax threw her hands up in frustration. "Maybe you wanted to impress me, make me feel small, or—"

"I was trying to help you, you idiot."

"What?"

She caught her breath, staring at him in the tight, four-walled little world where soft piped music played and, in the mirror on the rear wall, she could see the fury in her reflection.

"Sure. Yes, I know Paula," Lucas said defiantly. "Yes, my family does all that so-called rich people stuff you seem to have a bug up your ass about—as a matter of fact, we're building a new lab about ten minutes from here right now—but I thought that just made it easier. I figured it made it less awkward, like you could make it feel real, instead of just some stupid suck-up piece, and—"

"Then you should have *told* me!" Jax protested, even as her anger started to congeal into confusion. Why wasn't he mad at her? Why, after everything, every wrong foot and stupid misstep today, was he looking at her as if she'd hurt his feelings? She sighed. "I just... I'm sorry. I don't mean to be unprofessional, but...you made me look like an idiot."

Lucas scoffed and leaned back against the wall of the elevator. "No disrespect, but I think you did that yourself. I don't know what the hell you're so insecure about."

"What?"

The elevator juddered to a halt at the foyer level and the doors whisked open. Lucas shook his head and moved past her, a tightness around his eyes and mouth that spoke more of sore pride than annoyance.

"Let's just get to the car. If you can stand my presence long enough for a ride back to campus, that is."

Jax took a sharp breath in, catching the spicy scent of his cologne as he brushed against her. She had no idea how one person could be so infuriating...but she followed him anyway.

* * * *

In the car, Lucas switched on the radio, leaving a classical station on low to mask the awkward silence. Jax sighed, an uncomfortable sense of inevitability unfolding in her stomach.

"You don't have to do that."

"What?" he asked, shooting her a suspicious glance. The mid-morning sunlight cut across his face, making his dark eyes glitter with honey-gold flecks and highlighting the hard curves of his lips and cheekbones. "Maybe I just really like Schubert."

Jax smiled. "Nah. I see you more as a Dvorak kind of person. Maybe some Mahler. Big, complicated, sweeping things with swirly strings."

To her surprise, Lucas laughed—a real, deep, honest laugh that spilled from him with irrepressible grace.

"*Swirly strings*, huh? I had no idea you were a musicologist."

Jax shrugged, unable to keep a grin from breaking across her face. "Yeah, I changed my major. I know all the technical terms."

"So I see. You're pretty right, though."

"Really?"

"Yeah." He turned the Leaf around a corner that would take them downtown, instead of back onto the highway, the way they'd come. "I'm no big classical music expert, but I like the thoughtful, complex composers more than the super-dramatic virtuoso guys. How about you?"

"Some," Jax agreed. "When I was a kid, my grandpa used to play Stravinsky every Christmas. Some Grieg, some Holst... I took cello for a while, but I gave it up when I was about fifteen. Just didn't have time for it, not with school and jobs and stuff."

Lucas nodded, but left a beat of silence hanging between them.

It was Jax's turn then to snatch a look at him, watching his profile as he drove. A look of intense concentration etched his features, and there was something intimate and intense about sitting beside him. His car might not be strewn with personal detritus and daily mess, but it still seemed very *him*, and Jax was overcome by a feeling of swelling regret that she'd been so prickly, so quick to judge him.

She felt sure, if circumstances had been different that morning, she might have met this guy instead of the arch asshole who'd first greeted her...and she liked this version of Lucas a great deal.

"Listen," he said, the sound of his voice snatching her from her thoughts in a not entirely unpleasant shock, "I was an ass to you this morning. It was a bad day, a bad night, then getting called in like that... I shouldn't have taken it out on you, and I'm sorry we got off on the wrong foot. I can see how you'd think a lot of shit about me, especially given what people say. Would you like to go get coffee, maybe something to eat? We've got plenty of time before you need to get your story in for Dr. Reilly, so...c'mon. Lemme make it up to you, huh?"

Jax blinked and looked out of the car window. "Well, uh, since we're already pretty much *at* Starbucks..."

Lucas grinned. "I figured you wouldn't say no that way. Is that really bad?"

A couple of hours ago, his assumptions and his assholery would have pissed her off—this would have been the cherry on the top of a whole cupcake of annoyances—but Jax was either getting used to him or getting worn down by his insistence. The granola bar Ava had given her seemed as if it had been a very long time ago, too.

"All right, fine. I mean...yes. Thank you."

"Awesome. I know this really nice place. It's not far, just the other side of the Derham Bridge. You don't mind a shortcut, right?"

"Sure."

Jax watched Dalesburg's small, dated but quaint streets scroll by the window as he drove. She couldn't be sure, but it looked as if at least one boutique had a range of Cohan accessories in its window.

So much for illusions and expectations.

Chapter Three

Lucas drove them out past the edge of downtown, explaining that he'd found this new favorite spot while dropping in to check on the progress of the research lab his parents' company was building.

"It's a machine learning thing. The space used to be a warehouse, and it's full of crap still, but once everything's gutted, they're gonna renovate, use it for the R&D on these new projects, which I think is — "

"Hey. Look over there." Jax jerked upright in her seat, pointing across the rooflines of the red-brick industrial husks around them to where a dark plume of smoke was visible, twisting and curling against the sky. "Something's on fire."

Lucas pulled in and parked the Leaf. "Shit. Hey, you don't think — "

"There have been six fires in the industrial district in the past five months," Jax said, unlocking her phone. "Last one was about three days ago — they were covering the investigation in *The Recorder* this morning. Don't you even read the papers? They've ranged from pretty big blazes to just small ones, but the police think they were all intentionally set. They just haven't said whether it's one arsonist or multiple people."

She glanced at Lucas, aware of the look he was giving her.

"I'm impressed," he said. "You always just...carry around facts like that?"

Jax bristled. "As a matter of fact, yes. Facts are easy. It's making sense of them that can be hard. You know, there's no one around. We should see if anyone's called the fire department. If there's a building on fire back there—"

"Then we ought to be careful," Lucas said as she got out of the car. "Jax? Hey, wait! Did you hear me?"

She waved a hand. "Of course. Careful. Bring your camera, okay?"

"I— Damn it. Wait up!"

Jax didn't listen. She darted through a faded side street that led to where the smoke seemed to be coming from. They'd parked just a few blocks from the Derham Bridge, but this part of town was almost all disused warehouses and long-since-boarded-up factories, and everything seemed deserted. She glanced down at her phone, frowning as she realized there was no signal here. The smell of smoke hung on the air, acrid and dry.

"*Damn* it!" Lucas ran past her, his phone in his hand, and paused at the end of the alley. "I know where this is! This takes us up to the back of Wilson and Pike... I think that's our building. The lab. Fuck!"

He darted off around the corner and Jax followed, sticking with him along another few twists and turns through the crumbling brick maze. The Hargroves might have been doing their best to buy up and renovate a lot of Dalesburg's time-worn past, but there was still so much left standing vacant... It was something she'd been planning to write an article about at some point, Jax reflected ruefully. Some thoughtful piece about the decline of industry and the morals of big business.

She would have laughed at the irony, but at that moment they turned the corner and hit the back entrance of an old warehouse, which now had a Hargrove Industries—No Trespassing sign on its freight door. A side entrance stood ajar, and looked as if it had been forced, while smoke billowed from an upper-floor window.

"Ah, fuck," Lucas cursed, his hands in his hair. "Why aren't the alarms going off? I… Do you have a signal?"

Jax shook her head. Her phone was as good as dead.

"Shit. All right. I'm going to go in, pull the alarm manually, see if I can use one of the old landlines to call for help…if they still work. I don't know if they were taken out yet. The refurb's still in the early stages. Wait here, okay?"

"Are you crazy?" Jax grabbed at his arm, catching him around the wrist. "If somebody set that fire, they could still be in there. You could get hurt. Not to mention it's, y'know, a fucking burning building. Smart people don't just casually run into those!"

He gave her a mirthless grin. "I never really get accused of being smart."

"Lucas!" Jax watched, her stomach twisting into knots as he pulled away and ran for the side entrance. This was crazy. *He* was crazy. She groaned and bit her lip. She was crazy, too, wasn't she? She knew it. "Wait for me!"

* * * *

If the side streets had been a maze, the interior of the building was even more confusing. The paint on the brick and concrete walls was peeling, and tags had been scrawled in the innumerable corridors. Yet it was obviously under construction—here and there ladders and tools could be seen, and a faint aroma of paint and bleach hung over the pervading musty smell.

"Someone's been in here," Lucas said, keeping his voice hushed. "You should go. I don't want you to—"

"Fuck that," Jax whispered. "Where's the old manager's office? I'm guessing that's where the phone line and alarms are?"

He nodded and pointed to a door standing open at the end of the corridor. "We can cut through the storeroom back here. This is going to where the servers are when we're done. It leads straight to the office."

Lucas set his jaw and crept down the hallway. Jax followed. So far, she couldn't smell smoke or hear the fire's roar, but who the hell knew how long they had before the blaze took hold. She checked her phone, hoping it might show some sign of life, but the network still refused to cooperate.

Jax cursed and followed Lucas into the storeroom. Rows of boxes, no doubt left over from the building's previous use, lined the thick, peeling brick walls and, at the end of the long, narrow room, a small set of steps led up to a second door. It smelled a little musty in here, but Jax could see the traces of activity and refurbishment.

"So, this is the project your dad wants you to head up?" she asked, the pieces of understanding slipping into place. "The reason you'd rather stay at college?"

Lucas glanced at her, his mouth crumpling into a sheepish smile. "You could say that. I don't have a good head for business, though. I'd rather write about tech than get stuck competing against a dozen other start-ups for the same solution, especially when they don't have their families behind them. I guess you think that makes me a spoiled rich kid?"

"No." Jax edged past the heavy old door, with its rusty hinges and peeling paint, trying not to brush too hard against it. "I think it probably makes you a little more honest. And that's something to be proud of."

Lucas smiled at her and seemed about to say something, but then his mouth bowed into a look of horror...and the door swung shut behind them.

* * * *

"Damn it!" Lucas' palm slammed against the wall. "Both totally jammed. I can't believe this!"

He pushed back from the office door, unable to wrench open either of their escape options. They were stuck. Hopelessly, completely stuck.

"Anything?" he asked, nodding to Jax's phone.

She shook her head. "No signal, no Wi-Fi, no anything. It's like we're in a complete dead spot. You'd think an old place like this would be a little less impenetrable."

"Yeah." Lucas curled his lip. "If it burns down around us, maybe we'll be able to get a signal from the ashes."

Jax tried to smile, but the thought was a little too disquieting. She strained her ears, listening for an alarm, a siren—anything—but all she could make out was a faint creaking.

"What...?"She looked up at the storeroom's battered ceiling and its network of sprinklers. "Oh, no."

Jax winced as, with a lurching, grinding sound, the sprinklers came on, showering them with cold water at surprisingly high volume and pressure.

"Well, fuck," Lucas announced, trying to find somewhere dry to stash his camera bag. He glanced down at his shirt. "I guess we should be glad they've flushed the system recently. This is pretty not-gross for sprinkler water."

Jax stared up at him, her hair plastered to her cheeks. Water was running down her face, dripping from her lips and chin, and dampening her thin cotton shirt. She shivered, trying hard to keep her teeth from chattering.

"You're kidding me. You've *got* to be kidding. You're happy about this?"

"Best of a bad situation, right?" Lucas shrugged and gave her a sardonic smile. "I mean, usually sprinkler water's gross as hell. Even you'd be having a hard time looking cute if you were covered in brown sludge that's been sitting in the pipes for years."

His gaze dropped to the front of her shirt, now totally transparent and molded to her breasts, the lacy outline of her bra visible through the fabric. Jax folded her arms across her chest, more from irritation than self-consciousness.

Somehow, Lucas managed to look as if he'd just gone for a stroll in a pleasant spring rain. His hair was wet and tousled, the droplets of water misting his skin. His wet shirt hugged his broad arms and shoulders, and she tried not to stare at the little trails of moisture clinging to the bare arrow of his throat and sliding gently down the top of his chest.

"This is ridiculous," Jax growled, snatching away her gaze. "I can't believe we're stuck here. That this...this... God! I don't even know. I can't—"

"Hey. It's going to be okay."

"Is it?" she demanded. "I...I don't know what the hell happened. We're completely fucked. I—"

"Listen to me. It's going to be all right," Lucas insisted, coming forward to take hold of her shoulders, his big hands warm on her skin, the heat comforting through the chilled fabric of her shirt. "Whatever crazy firebug broke in here and screwed with things, someone's going to call the fire department. They're going to come and put it out, and get us out of here. Okay? It's a small, contained fire. We're gonna be okay. The sprinklers are going off because the whole building is on a single system — like in dorms. You're really going to stand there and tell me the sprinklers never went off once in your dorm?"

Jax let out a long breath. She knew what he was doing, but he was doing it well, and she could feel her panic dissipating. She dredged up a thin, damp smile.

"Well…yeah. And for totally no reason. I hardly even burned the toast."

Lucas grinned, shaking his head. "It would be you, wouldn't it? Always you."

"I… I'm scared," she whispered, choking the admission out between chattering teeth and hating the way she could feel pressure building behind her eyes. She would *not* cry in front of him. Not over this. Not here. "And…and I'm cold. And pissed off. I can't believe we got into this mess, and…and I'm sorry. Sorry I dragged you into it. All of this, it's my fault. I just… I wanted so bad to…to —"

"I know," he said quietly. "I know, Jax. It's okay."

She looked up, wary at the absence of mockery in his tone.

"It's okay," Lucas murmured again, squeezing her shoulders. "It's all right. We're in this together, and we're going to be okay."

With the last of her determination, Jax choked back a sob. His touch was so assured and full of promise…promises she was so desperate to believe.

Jax looked up at him. His eyes were dark and soft, for once devoid of all that sparkling laughter and spiky teasing, and she'd never seen him so gentle. She unfolded her arms, letting them fall to her sides, and her lips worked around a few empty words. What could she say? That this had all been a huge fuck-up, that she'd messed up again and she was sorry? She was so, so tired of being sorry. So tired of being wrong.

As Lucas' broad palm rubbed warmth into her arm, she felt an answering heat wash through every part of her. She wanted this…him. She wanted things to be right, just for once.

Jax reached out, letting her touch trail against the wet skin of his arms, up to the rolled sleeves and damp, clinging cotton of his shirt, wordless questions hanging from her fingertips. She didn't quite dare look him in the face, but she could hear the change in his breathing.

Lucas pulled her close, wrapping his arms around her, and she pressed against him, her head tucked beneath his chin. His chest was broad, solid, and she inhaled, pulling in so much of that heady, earthy scent of his that her lungs were full of him, blotting out everything else. There was just this, just the warmth of his arms, his strength wrapped around her, and that blend of soap and the rich, spicy, citrus-laced cologne he wore, mixed with the tantalizing sharpness of sweat and the indescribable extra something that was just *him*.

"It's all right," Lucas promised, holding her close as he stroked her hair, one arm clutched fiercely around her shoulders. "It's all right."

His voice was low, roughened a little. Jax wondered if it was fear, or the same urgent need that was uncoiling in her belly. Her nipples peaked, chafing against the rough wetness of her bra, and she shifted, desperate to be closer to him and all he offered. She tilted her head, bringing her lips level with his neck. His pulse beat hard and firm there, his skin smooth and warm, and the sheer intensity of his proximity overwhelmed her, sending her spiraling into dizzying shivers of want.

Jax kissed him softly, just pressing her lips against his throat in a gentle yet insistent offer. She felt his breath catch, then he pulled back a little, staring down at her.

"Jax...?"

"Sorry," she whispered, aware of how small and breathy her voice sounded. She knew she looked like a wet, bedraggled mess, too, eyeliner smeared and her hair in ruins.

Lucas' expression fell somewhere between disbelief and confusion, but she could see something else burning in his eyes—a light of recognition, and of desire.

"Sorry?" A dry breath of laughter slipped over his lips. "You're ridiculous."

Jax's mouth crumpled. "Oh. Thanks."

"Stop it." His arms tightened around her, his voice a low but irresistible warning that hummed right to her core. "You know what I mean. Don't be sorry. You're gorgeous, funny, smart...interesting. I could spend hours just digging into that head of yours, finding out what makes you work the way you do. I'm going to," he added, squeezing her waist for emphasis, "when we get out of here. You know that, right?"

Jax smiled. The prospect wasn't as terrible as she might have imagined. "I can live with that."

Lucas returned her smile with a look of warmth that made her tremble, and she couldn't dispel the gnawing need inside her. Jax pressed closer, bringing her mouth to his and feeling his breath against her lips.

She felt the shift in his body—the tension and eagerness in him—and knew he felt it just as strongly as she did. Lucas swallowed, the muscles of his throat flexing. Jax stared, unable to think of anything but running her tongue along that hard column and kissing the stubble-specked line of his jaw.

"Are you sure you want this?" he asked, his voice a rough whisper.

She nodded. "Yes. I want to. I want *you*. Hell, it's not every day you get trapped alone with the hottest guy on campus, is it?"

Lucas looked at her in wonder, a laugh caught between his teeth. Droplets of water beaded both their faces — she couldn't stop staring at the way it clung to his tan skin, one rivulet hugging his full lower lip in the most tantalizing way.

Jax felt the same wetness on her own lips, and — as Lucas cupped her face in his hands — her mouth burned where his thumb rubbed across it, wiping the water away with the same ease that he'd fixed her hair in the car that morning. This time, though, it didn't feel like an invasion, a liberty she hadn't expected. It felt right, the way she knew being in his hands *could* feel, and she wanted that. She wanted to share his certainty, his strength… Just for a little while.

Jax parted her lips a little as she gazed up at him, her body responding to his touch with no thought, no question. It was almost too easy, and for a second she almost balked at it. Perhaps he did always get what he wanted, and she knew he wanted her. She could see it now, seared into his eyes, and the knowledge made her feel at once powerful and so small, like a flower facing a tornado.

Lucas cupped her face in his hands, those strong fingers tilting her head back, and kissed her, and the uncertainty began to melt away, replaced by the easy comfort of his strength. There was no hesitation now, that gentle, tentative inquisitiveness forgotten. His touch was decisive, his mouth covering hers in one quick, hungry movement, and Jax let out a soft moan. If she'd doubted before that he meant it, there was no confusion now — he wanted her, and he meant to have her.

She opened to him at once, his tongue a thread of flame that parted her lips and sought out her secrets, accepting neither resistance nor half measures. He kissed hard, rough, taking the breath from her body and the strength from her knees as he claimed her in a relentless, eager rhythm.

"Here."

His strong hands around her waist, he lifted her up onto one of the stacks of boxes, which wobbled a little as Jax braced herself against it. Lucas leaned in to kiss her again, and she wrapped her arms around his neck, burying her fingers in his wet hair. She pulled him close, not wanting to let him go. They were at an equal height now, and she could explore him as much as she wanted...but he leaned back, making her wait.

"You gotta be patient," he said as he rubbed his thumb across her lips. "Always so goddamn eager to do things your own way, aren't you?"

Jax nipped at the pad of flesh before pulling his thumb into her mouth and sucking on it, entranced by the smoke-salt flavor of his skin. She kept eye contact as she did so and watched the look of strained desire that sluiced across his features, darkening his expression and making his mouth tense.

"My way's good," she said innocently as she released his thumb. "Isn't it?"

Lucas gave her a harsh, tight kind of smile as he slipped his fingers into her hair, taking a firm hold at the back of her head. He moved his other hand to the hem of her skirt, which he began to push up, revealing the soft, sheer gray of her pantyhose.

"Very nice," he said before kissing her again, slow and deep, as he stroked her thighs, his strong fingers traveling farther up with every touch.

Jax squirmed, caught between his wicked hands teasing her and offering that delicious tugging on her hair, and the hypnotic thrall of his mouth. Desire burned under her skin until she was surprised the water didn't turn to steam between them, and she held her breath as Lucas' warm, insistent touch was right there, right where she wanted him, at the juncture of her thighs.

"Oh," she murmured, feeling his fingertips just graze her underwear through the pantyhose. "Fuck."

"I told you," he said, planting a kiss on her forehead, "be patient. Now, how attached are you to these pantyhose?"

"What?" Jax frowned. She'd been kissed into incomprehension, and all she wanted was to be touched. She pressed against him, feeling his fingers tighten on her inner thigh, and realization slipped over her. "Oh. Yeah, not at all."

Lucas let out a breath of relief. "Good."

His hand left her hair for a moment as he reached down. Jax spread her legs and he pushed her skirt up the rest of the way, then ripped a hole in her pantyhose. The sheer, flimsy fabric gave way in his hands, tearing along the length of her thigh and leaving her bared and open to him, nothing between them but the white cotton of her panties. With some last shred of self-consciousness, Jax knew her wetness must already be blossoming there, darkening the fabric with her desperation. She didn't care. She didn't care about anything anymore, as long as he touched her.

"Fuck, you're beautiful," Lucas murmured, trailing a teasing fingertip up and down that strip of dampened cotton. "Look at you. So wet for me."

Jax's eyes fluttered closed, her breath coming high and fast in her chest. She bit her lip, aware of his hands on her body, his wide palms covering her shoulders. He kissed her neck and up to the point of her jaw, his lips brushing against the dolphin earring he'd noticed earlier. He chuckled, and his breath skimmed her skin, stirring a deep surge of want within her.

"I'd love to see you on a beach," Lucas murmured, trailing his fingers down to the buttons of her shirt, popping each one with a slow determination that made Jax wish he'd just rip the damn thing open. "Taste the salt on your skin. Kiss you in the sunshine and fuck you in the surf."

She smiled, knotting her fingers in his hair as he nipped at the hollow beneath the point of her jaw. She'd never have taken him for such a romantic, but she wasn't about to argue. For a moment, memories of vacations back home filtered through Jax's mind, and she could almost feel the sun on her shoulders and the breeze on her face, sand between her toes and the sound of waves calling her to the shore.

Lucas pushed her shirt open and tugged down her white lace bra, exposing her breasts to the cold, clammy air, and a gasp caught in Jax's throat. He bent low, his lips and the light stubble on his chin teasing her nipples as he greeted each in turn with a low moan of approval. She exhaled, the memories of sand and sunshine falling away to leave the delicious wet heat of his mouth and the damp chill of this strange, bare room. It all seemed so wrong — so hushed, desperate, and forbidden — but the thought of that only thrilled her more.

For all Jax knew, somewhere upstairs the fire was still burning. She had yet to hear sirens outside. They were trapped, stuck here together, and the rest of the world didn't matter. Right now, right here, a whole other inferno was blazing, and there was an odd energy in Lucas' touch that at once soothed and excited her. She felt sure she'd gone crazy—this was insane, wasn't it?—but if she *was* crazy, she might as well do something wild and take pleasure in it. She was already lost, carried away by desire, and she didn't mind one little bit.

Lucas pushed her panties aside, and she trembled in anticipation at the thought of having those long, strong fingers finally within her, but she should have known better. This was Lucas Hargrove, the man who got the biggest kick in the world out of teasing her with a joke or a wink, and he wasn't going to stop there. His fingertips barely grazed her, the frustration dragging a broken moan of resentment from deep in Jax's chest.

"Fucking touch me," she pleaded, her hips bucking as she fought to get closer to him without losing her unsteady perch on the boxes.

Lucas just smiled and slid his hand back into her hair. He wound his fingers into the wet red tresses, settling deep at the roots. He tugged as he kissed her again, drawing it out until he was sucking at her lower lip and turning her mind into one blank white wall of static.

"This what you want?" he asked, his lips against her cheek and his voice a low rumble against her skin as—finally—he pressed one fingertip between her folds, rubbing at her with slow, steady strokes.

Jax screwed her eyes tight shut. Her nipples stood out like pebbles in the cold air, her skin wet and chilled, torn between the contrast of the room and the inferno blazing inside her. Any thoughts left in her head coalesced into one bright stream of need, and she didn't dare open her mouth, afraid of what she'd promise.

Lucas trailed his index finger up her lips, settling just below the hard, slick knot of her clit. Jax shivered, her hips shifting in small, needy circles, yet he somehow managed to keep dodging her.

"Hold still," he said, his breath hot against her cheek as he tugged her hair in a gentle yet firm warning. "There's no rush, baby."

Jax whimpered. "But… I want… I *need*… Please?"

"No."

The word was a ghost on her skin, dragging another desperate moan from her throat. He eased back, and she knew she had no choice. She obeyed, stilling her movements and tensing up as he flicked the lightest feather of a fingertip across her clit. Beads of sweat broke along her spine, and Jax clenched her teeth, quivering with the maddening frustration.

Lucas leaned his touch a little farther in, the wide, warm tip of his finger resting against her sensitive flesh. The contact was electric, sending shivers of pleasure arcing through her body, and she flexed against him, her clit pulsing with the ache of pent-up need.

"Touch me," she begged. "Hard. I like it hard. Rub my clit… I need it. Please."

Lucas gave a soft laugh, his lips grazing her temple. "For fuck's sake, Jax. Really? You're *still* trying to tell me what to do?"

She groaned, caught somewhere between rage, frustration and relief that—even in the middle of all this—he was still himself. If she'd been thinking clearly, the slightest bit of joy at his mockery would have surprised and even mortified her, but Jax was long past caring. She turned her head as best she could and burrowed into his neck with a soft cry of yearning.

It was apparently all the admission, all the supplication he needed. Lucas' touch danced on her clit, spinning irresistible circles as light as a cobweb. Jax groaned into his chest, frustration and desire warring inside her as the cruelest of pleasure built.

This wasn't how she touched herself, or the way she liked lovers to touch her. She wanted to know she was fucking, to have a man's hands on her with uncompromising surety. She wanted her clit rubbed hard, rough, until she broke against the wall of pleasure like a wave. This was different. This pleasure was half torture, demanding effort from her to follow the teasing threads of his touch, to work at keeping time with the sensations he used to torment her...and it was intoxicating.

Heat welled deep inside her and Jax trembled, clinging to Lucas to stop herself from falling. So much—too much—was centered on that one needle-sharp point, that place his skin met hers and laid claim to her. Somewhere in her addled brain, the thought that she wouldn't like it fizzled and died, and a kind of raw, urgent want rose, coalescing every shred of awareness Jax had into that single wet jewel beneath Lucas' fingers.

"Stop," she muttered, as his wicked touch spiraled faster, so gentle that it was impossible to believe it could feel so good. "Please...."

"Do you mean that?"

His arms were so strong around her, cradling her even as he tugged again at her hair. Jax melted into him, into the pressure and into the sweet, burning delight between her legs. She flexed her fingers against his chest and shook her head.

"N-No. No. I just... I didn't want to come yet. I... Oh, fuck, you're gonna make me come..."

"Good," he whispered, increasing the pace of those devilish fingers. "Finally, you're going to do something you're told. Come for me, baby."

His voice struck a nerve at Jax's core, that low masculine purr turning her belly to liquid as it burned a path from her brain to her clit. A choked, high-pitched squeal broke from her lips as the world turned white and starlit, and she spilled into oblivion in his hands, coming harder and harder with every last flick of his fingers against her. He didn't stop—wouldn't stop—as she bucked against him. She clenched her hands in the folds of his shirt and her face buried in his chest, and she at once hated and loved him for it.

"Such a good girl," Lucas murmured, stroking her cheek with his thumb.

His other hand, still resting between her legs, caressed the soft skin of her inner thigh, brushing against the hole he'd torn in her pantyhose. Jax shivered, breathless and balanced somewhere between bliss and hunger. She had never felt at once so vulnerable and so powerful, the center of someone's world even as she was broken down and made so deliciously dirty.

She tugged at Lucas' shirt, pulling him down for a kiss. He obliged, and the taste of him filled her, his hot, supple tongue teasing hers with an eager, relentless drive. He slid his fingers down her throat, gliding over her collarbone before slipping down to tease her nipple, his touch hungry and possessive. The contact had her shivering all over again, pushing into his touch. Lucas cupped her breast in his hand, and Jax felt her nipple harden, peaking against his palm. He groaned into her mouth as he squeezed and rolled her breast, sending a fresh wave of desire through her and opening a burning ache right at her core.

"I want you inside me," she murmured against Lucas' lips. "Please?"

He let out a low moan, the sound of it humming through her like an impatient, desperate growl, and she could tell how hard he'd been holding back. He pulled away just enough to study her, the look in his dark eyes heavy with a blend of lust and determination that told her — if she gave herself to him — there would be no turning back.

Somehow, that no longer seemed like a warning worth heeding.

"Sure?" Lucas asked, the edge of his thumb rubbing across her jaw as if he was committing every detail of her face to memory.

Jax nodded. She couldn't remember being more sure of anything. "Do you have…?"

"In my wallet. Hold on. Don't move," Lucas added, smirking at her as he pulled away to retrieve the condom.

Jax raised an eyebrow, but she was fresh out of clever things to say. The loss of his presence was like a sudden pain, leaving her cold, abandoned…and very aware of her sudden ridiculousness. She looked down at herself, her skirt hiked up and her pantyhose torn to shreds, one pump hanging off her foot and her clothes wet through and rumpled. She'd never felt like such a slut. Hell, maybe that was what she was. After all, it was hard to believe, but she was balanced on a stack of damp boxes in a storeroom that smelled of smoke, the threat of mortal peril still fraying her nerves, and what did she want more than anything?

She watched Lucas unbutton his pants, pushing his designer jeans and black shorts down to mid-thigh to reveal a startlingly beautiful, achingly hard, tantalizingly smooth, thick cock…and, in some primal, hungry place in her brain, the whole world made a little more sense.

"Oh," Jax murmured.

Lucas grinned at her — a feral, predatory expression that said he'd waited long enough — and she felt her body respond, heat blossoming in her cheeks at being the object of such greedy interest, even as an answering flame licked at the core of her belly and made her clit leap all over again.

He closed the distance between them, snatching her up into another of those deep, rough kisses as he tore the hole in her pantyhose wider. Jax squirmed as she felt the fabric rip, straining for a second against her skin before baring her to the air. She couldn't remember ever being this wet, this desperate to be filled. He was teasing her, rubbing the fat head of his cock along her folds until she groaned into his mouth.

"Oh, come *on*," she said between kisses, as he nipped at the point of her chin. "The fucking building's on fire, Lucas. You don't have time to tease me."

He laughed, the sound low and warm against her skin. "Yeah? Maybe it's the perfect time for teasing. If we're trapped down here until the fire crew puts the whole place out, just think how long I've got to drive you crazy."

Jax screwed her eyes shut as his smart goddamn mouth closed on her neck.

"You're an asshole. You know that, right?"

Lucas' lips seared a path up her throat, ending just beneath her ear.

"Uh-huh," he murmured, and thrust hard inside her.

Jax squealed and clung to him, the sensation of being so easily and uncompromisingly filled sending fireworks exploding in her brain. He waited, giving her time until she tipped her head back, surrendering to the feeling and to the powerful ache that only he could help make better.

"Fuck me," she pleaded, wrapping her legs around his waist and peering up at him, already hazy with desire. "Fuck me into the fucking ashes."

Lucas groaned, moving his hands up her body, skimming over the mess he'd made of her skirt and shirt, cupping the curves of her ass and hips before traveling up her ribs to take hold of her breasts. He couldn't seem to touch her enough, and she reveled in his eagerness as he surged within her. He lowered his head, and Jax gasped at the warmth of his tongue on her chilled, hard nipple, wet heat engulfing her as he kissed, licked and sucked at the tender flesh.

"You're so fucking hot," Lucas murmured, kissing his way across to her other nipple and pulling her back into that merciless tangle of teeth and tongue that had Jax arching into his lips, flooded with the warmth of pleasure. "So beautiful."

Jax groaned, losing herself to the heat and hunger of his touch. He moved within her, slow and heavy as he sucked harder at her nipple, and her mind was blank but for the feeling of how full she felt, how hot and right it was.

As Lucas kissed his way up her throat and moved his hand back to her hair, knotting his fingers deep at the roots, little thoughts batted at her. The distant reality of the situation—the smoke, the alarms, the gray concrete around them, and the patter of sprinkler water on their bodies—seemed little more than a dream, and she couldn't force it to feel real. Yet, when she closed her eyes, there was a small voice at the back of her mind, the last trace of coherent thought that told her what they were doing was crazy. There was a fire, the building was burning… This was nuts.

Images of smoke coiling down the stairwells and firefighters breaking their way through the boarded-up windows played in Jax's mind. And what would they find when they smashed down the doors? Two horny kids fucking in the basement.

She felt sure she should be embarrassed, humiliated, ashamed of herself and of this lapse in control, but Lucas' hands felt so big and warm on her hips, and his thick cock stretched her walls with a practiced ease that made stars burst behind her eyes. Pleasure built in molten waves at her center. Somehow, that last whisper of fear just became part of the fantasy, and Jax spread her legs wide, pulling him deeper. She wanted them to see. Anyone who came in here should see—she was wanton, powerful, a goddess riding waves of desire, and the big, beautiful man between her thighs was at once her jewel and her conqueror.

He flexed, driving his cock deeper on every thrust, and Jax moaned as the pleasure built at her core. He teased her a little, pulling almost all the way out before filling her again, driving her crazy and making her beg for him, beg to be fucked deeper and harder.

Lucas, keen to fulfill that request, turned her so she faced the boxes, her bare breasts crushed against the damp cardboard she was bent over, and guided her left leg up into a foothold. Jax closed her eyes at the feel of his hands running over her ass, his warm, strong fingers claiming her body and burning a path wherever he touched.

"Please," she murmured. She missed him too much, needed him too badly. "Give it to me? I want it."

Lucas' hands were on her hips then, the hard heat of his cock pressing between her thighs and making her pussy flutter with the ache of anticipation.

"What?" he asked, his tone light and teasing, though she could hear the strain beneath the word. "Tell me. Tell me what you want. I want to hear it again."

If she hadn't been so desperate, she'd have enjoyed knowing how much he loved her desire for him, but Jax's needs were screaming for satisfaction, and she struggled to get the words out.

She wriggled a little, drawing a flinch from him even as her knees grew weak.

"I want your cock inside me," she said, hearing the breath catch in his throat. "I want you to pound the fuck out of me and rub my clit until I come all over that fat fucking cock. Sound good?"

Lucas' breath was hot on her nape, the hardness of his chest pressed against her back and his arm strong around her ribs. Yet, for all his masculine power, she felt the way he trembled against her, and heard the quiver in his voice as it rumbled against her skin.

"Oh, you're gonna get what you want," he said, dragging his lips across her shoulder and up her neck in a trail of rough kisses, his breath coming hot and fast on her skin. "I don't know where the hell you've been all my life, but I know what you need. This is what you need, isn't it, baby?"

As he spoke, he thrust into her in one hot, easy movement. Jax sighed, trembling a little as he hit every sweet spot she had in the first of those long, hard strokes. She leaned her head back, finding him answering at once in the way his fingers wound into her hair, giving a slow, strong tug. She arched her back, felt his other hand at the front of her waist, supporting her as he began to move, and she was lost to the rhythm he set, breaking apart on the feeling of his heat filling her, fucking her, making her over everywhere he touched.

"Fuck," she breathed, the word a tremulous chant on her lips. "Oh, fuck…"

Lucas did just that. He fucked her until she was moaning his name, the boxes rocking and creaking beneath her, and those irrefutable waves of pleasure were building from the ends of her fingers to the tips of her water-stained pumps.

"Let me feel it," he whispered, reaching around to touch her as he moved, his big, warm hand cupping her belly before he trailed his fingers down toward her clit. "Let me feel you come, baby."

Lucas rubbed her clit as he fucked her, and Jax stifled a scream, caught between the ruthless pleasure he wrung from her and the deep waves of bliss that came with every hard thrust. She ached for him, to be filled over and over as he took her, his every stroke hitting something dark and primal inside her. When he pulled her hair again, she arched back against him, a growl on her lips and her whole body a quivering bow. He'd made her into both his toy and his weapon, ready to be the instrument of either destruction or delight, and all Jax could do was exist on that shivering edge of pleasure.

Lucas moved his fingers faster as he fucked her deeper, the gentle circles becoming rough, ragged touches. He swelled inside her, their breathing knitted together in hungry gasps and pants, mirrored by the sounds of their bodies moving in an ever more desperate rhythm.

The pleasure built in wave after wave, pushing Jax higher and higher until her whole body thrummed and ached with it. She couldn't have held back if she'd wanted to, and Lucas certainly had no intention of letting her. With the breath all but knocked from her, a series of desperate squeals on her lips and his beautiful cock relentlessly caressing her G-spot, Jax broke on the tidal surge of bliss that coursed through her, coming in a splintering orgasm that exploded from her very center and just didn't seem to stop.

Lucas kept his fingers on her clit, driving her further as molten pleasure flowed from the soles of her feet through to the top of her head. She shook, obliterated and shattered on the sparkling edges of pleasure that held her in its grasp like a glass crown, shard-like and glittering.

She was aware of crying out, of her moans and shrill gasps, and of Lucas tightening his hold on her, his movements growing erratic and desperate as he groaned out his own climax. He gave one final thrust, and collapsed against Jax's back, his breath grazing her wet skin as they panted together, finding their way back to earth, yet still tangled blissfully together.

Chapter Four

"I can't believe we did that," Jax said, looking up at the sprinklers, which were still dripping a little. "Can you?"

They were sitting together at the foot of the storeroom boxes, clothing more or less rearranged, and Lucas' arm was around her shoulders.

Lucas smirked. "No. Why? You regret it?"

"Fuck no," Jax said, much blunter than she'd intended, sending them both giggling. "I mean—"

"See?" Lucas said, recovering his composure. "That's what's amazing about you. You're so...*real*. I love it. No matter what, it's just *there*."

Jax looked at him in surprise. "Oh? As opposed to...?"

"You know." He shrugged. "Not saying what you mean. Hiding what you think. At first, I thought that's what you were like, but you're not. You're so much yourself...and I like that girl."

"Oh." A small smile tugged at the corner of Jax's lips. "Well, that girl kinda likes you too. You're not the prissy rich boy asshole I thought you were."

"Truly?" Lucas grinned, affecting an old-fashioned transatlantic accent. "How charming! Why, thank you, Ms. North!"

Jax snorted. "Shut the fuck up."

They both laughed, and he dragged her into a sideways hug that spilled into his lap and, from there, a sprawled and awkward kiss. Jax let her fingers tangle in Lucas' curls and smiled. He was so very handsome.

"Jax?"

"Hmm?"

"Listen."

A look of worry flitted across Lucas' face, and Jax pushed herself up on one elbow, straining her ears. He was right—beyond the windowless walls of the storeroom, and the still-dripping sprinklers and their creaking pipes, Jax could hear the sound of sirens. Fire engines, police... Help was on the way.

She gasped, half in relief and half in the sudden realization of what that meant.

"Holy shit. Did we just do it in a crime scene?"

"Yeah," Lucas said, nodding. "Pretty sure we did. You know we're probably going to have to give statements, explain what we're doing here... Try to get people to believe it's not my fault."

Jax bit her lip. He had a point. His family's name was on the side of the building—it wouldn't be a stretch for anyone to assume insurance fraud. She pushed her fingers through her wet hair.

"It's going to be okay. There's not going to be any evidence tying you to the fire—you didn't go anywhere near it. If anyone thinks differently, well, we'll cross that bridge when we come to it. Right now, we're going to get out of here, you're gonna take some fucking *killer* pictures of the scene, and you and I are going to have *so* much more than an interview with a college donor to file for the paper."

He looked up at her, his expression a blend of admiration and surprise, and smiled. "God, you really know how to turn a situation to your advantage, don't you?"

Jax grinned. "I rather thought that's what we did here. Don't you agree?"

Lucas' smile broadened, a flush of color touching his cheeks. "I guess you could say that. Okay. Ready to face the chaos out there?"

She nodded. "With you, yes. I think so."

"Hold on." Lucas took hold of her shoulder and held her still as he hooked his fingers into her hair, readjusting and tidying it again. His touch lingered, fingertips trailing down her cheek when he was done. "There. Gorgeous."

Jax smiled, warmth flushing through her. No matter how chaotic and disheveled she was, she felt beautiful with him.

"So, uh, after we've got through this mess," Lucas suggested, "called in the news to Dr. Reilly, and maybe gone a little way toward explaining what the hell happened here today... D'you feel like maybe getting dinner?"

Jax smirked. "Really? I thought wining and dining me was supposed to come first."

His eyes twinkled with mirth. "Bullshit, North. I already made sure you came first, and *that* is because I'm a gentleman."

Laughter spilled from her, perfectly uncontained and free.

"Hmm." She pursed her lips, pretending to consider Lucas' proposal. "How about we go back to your place, order pizza, and I can type up my story and email it in for tomorrow's first edition before we, uh, go over all the events and compare our notes?"

Lucas nodded, a glint of mischief shining in his face. "Ah. I see. Rigorous attention to detail. Very good."

"Absolutely. It's best practice, I think. Making sure we've covered the story from *every* angle."

He grinned, an adorable hint of color rising in his cheeks as he stared at her. An answering heat swelled within her, and Jax couldn't help but begin to imagine all the delights still to come. She wanted to see Lucas Hargrove completely naked, every inch of him bared for her to explore. There were still so many new things between them. So what if they'd had an unconventional start? Maybe it'd burn out in a couple of days, and they would both go back to their lives. Or, just maybe, it might take them both somewhere interesting.

Jax had no idea which was more likely, and — for once, despite all her best-laid plans — the uncertainty was rather thrilling.

"There's one thing, though," she said, as a stab of guilty recollection speared her brain. "Can we get a veggie supreme sent over to 1148 Blake Court?"

Lucas quirked an eyebrow. "Forget to feed your fish?"

"Ha ha, funny. No, my roommate. I promised to pick one up, and I can't leave her feeling completely forgotten."

He grinned, affecting that cocky smirk once again. "Well, y'know, if she's hot, we could always invite — "

"Pig!" Jax teased, nudging his shoulder with her own.

"Kidding! Kidding!" Lucas held up his hands in a gesture of innocence. "Honest. Listen, are you sure you can skip out on her? Because if — "

"She'll understand," Jax said, watching the way his lips moved and thinking of all the plans she had for them. "Besides, how often does a story like this come up, huh?"

A smile spread across Lucas' face. "Well, it's been one for the portfolio."

"Damn straight," Jax agreed as she leaned close to seize his mouth in a long, deep kiss.

This was one story she definitely wanted to capture in detail, word by word, and print in the fullest edition possible.

CHASING
CHARLIE

Dedication

This one is for the late, great Doris O'Connor and
our friends, The RavDor Chicks.
And the lovely husband, Paul of course.

Chapter One

A red nose and freezing ears were not the best look. Especially when she wanted to appear cool, calm and collected and not at all bothered that instead of heading to uni in Hong Kong, across the harbor on the Star Ferry with her mates, she was standing in the freezing cold, waiting for the local bus back on the east coast of Scotland. Without any mates.

Life and its bloody curve balls.

Charlotte Xiǎo Méihuā — phonetically Shu-Mai — Allsop, usually known as Charlie, stamped her feet to try to keep the circulation going and swore under her breath. Who on earth thought it a good idea not to bring hat and gloves out? It might say it was only autumn on the calendar, but no one had told the east coast of Scotland that. The uni playing fields which she passed on her walk to the nearest bus stop were white, and the pond nearby appeared as if it would freeze you if you went within three feet of it. Not that she intended to. She preferred to swim in warm and probably chlorinated, or salty, water. For one wistful moment she allowed herself to remember

Big Wave Beach in Hong Kong, and long, hot, fun-filled days with her mates. One in particular, but that was over now, with no regrets. It was as they say — good while it lasted — but it wouldn't have lasted much longer, even if she hadn't moved away again.

Charlie blew on her fingers — it made no difference, and she suspected her nose was blue with cold because her hands were white. All she needed was something red and she could have a job imitating a flag!

Great look — not.

Why the hell had she chosen to live where she did? Okay nice house, great garden and independence, but shit, maybe she should have said sod it and found a flat share.

When would the bloody bus arrive? She'd been told it left at ten past and it was almost that now. Charlie stuffed her hands into her pockets and glanced around. Two girls, both in padded jackets and woolly hats, were huddled together giggling over something on one of their phones. Three boys — without padded jackets or hats and without blue noses — had given her the once-over then ignored her. Much to her relief. She was too cold to think of any good put-downs or pithy comments.

As they were all standing around in the same area, she had to assume they were all waiting for the now overdue bus. One of the halls of residence wasn't far away.

"Hi, no bus yet?"

Charlie swung around to see a newcomer — female, thank goodness — behind her. She shook her head. "Nope. I was told ten past."

The newcomer, tall and redheaded like Charlie herself, shrugged. "Ten past is a moveable time when it comes to good old Duckman's Coaches. It's turned up anytime from five past to twenty-five to, with no reason why. They're quacking shite. The one they send us is as old as I am, I swear. It's broken down on the way, run out of petrol twice, leaked rusty water all over my unsuspecting brother and had a window fall out halfway over the bumps. You know where the local council in its infinite wisdom decided to do traffic calming measures without realizing it's probably the least used street in town. The joys of living on the outskirts of town and getting the worst bus service in the world. I'm guessing you're new, or at least new to the joys of Duckman's. I'm Lily Bannerman, by the way. *Are* you new, or have I just never met you?"

Charlie took a swift glance at the pleasant-sounding girl next to her. Her long, red hair was almost covered by an overlarge woolly hat and she was another one who wore a padded jacket and a pair of gloves. Sensible.

At least I've got the jacket. She'd been tempted not to bother, but thank goodness her mum had put her foot down with, *'If you get pneumonia, I'll have to look after you. You're a rotten patient.'* Both true.

"New to this part of town. Did my last year at a uni in Hong Kong, you know, like we can?"

Lily nodded.

"I moved to this part of town last week, after the place I was due to live in was flooded because some numpty in the upper flat left the bath tap on. Thank goodness it was the cold one," Charlie explained, glad someone acknowledged her existence. "I was due to move soon anyway, but I just brought the date forward and accepted I'm living in a building site for now." Her new house was not quite finished, but, thanks to a sum of money handed to her by her beloved godmother, she had been able to buy it and move in before the kitchen cupboards had handles on and the downstairs loo a door. She held out her hand, used to the politeness of Hong Kong. "Charlie Allsop. I'm doing French and Mandarin. Hi."

"Mandarin?" Lily's eyebrows disappeared behind her fringe as she returned the handshake. "Wow. Isn't that hard?"

Charlie shrugged, a bit embarrassed she might have sounded as if she were boasting. She hadn't meant to. "Probably, but I lived in Hong Kong, as a teen, so I've got the basics." She had more than that, but wasn't going to show off, or explain she could get by in Cantonese as well.

"Wow again. And now bonny Scotland. Chalk and cheese. Why?" Lily sounded genuinely interested and not merely nosy. She stamped her feet. "This weather is the pits. Sorry, go on."

Charlie smiled. "You've got it right about the weather, though they're just coming out of typhoon season over there, which can be pretty hairy. Long story. Short version, I was born here, we moved to Shanghai when I was around a year old, Singapore when I was three, then California and then Hong Kong for the last seven years."

"Scotland instead of Hong Kong? Why?"

She shrugged. "Who knows? I got a place to study in Hong Kong or Beijing if I wanted one, but Hong Kong would have meant living at home for a while and Beijing…hmm." She wriggled her nose. "I love the city, but I didn't want to study there and this uni has a great reputation. Plus, I knew I could do my overseas year in Hong Kong if I wanted to."

"Bit of a culture shock, though?"

"You can say that again."

Lily shivered. "How about our balmy weather, eh?"

"Weather-wise is a shock as well. Where's the season of mists and mellow fruitfulness my mum waffles on nostalgically about?"

"Missed us out this year, as it often does. The weather is pants, I agree," Lily said with an exaggerated shudder.

"I'm not sure you ever get used to winter lasting ten months, or that's what it feels like. Seriously, it was gorgeous for two or three months last summer. This year, we've had about two or three weeks. One of those in April." She rolled her eyes. "I remember my mum saying they all wore short long johns — if that's not a misnomer — under their skirts years ago. I wish we still did. Mind you, leggings under trousers work. Weather apart, though, we're not that bad when you get to know us," Lily said as she glanced around. "Well, most of us, anyway. Some just can't help being assholes. But you'd know that from when you were here before, I guess?"

Charlie grinned. "I was too young, but males are the same the world over."

One of the three boys in a huddle appeared to notice her for the first time. "Oy, Lil," he bellowed. "Who's our mate? Where's Jake then? Having a quick fag before he eats a mint and tells you he doesn't smoke?"

"As I was saying," Lily muttered under her breath. She raised her voice. "My mate? Hands off. About Jake? Your guess is as good as mine, Hamish. We left together. My brother is the one he's yabbering about," she explained to Charlie. "Doesn't smoke 'cause he's a rugby fanatic, but those idiots like to pretend he does. He makes a point of never hanging around here, and rolls up as the bus does on the days he has to catch it. Never missed it yet, but one time…"

The boy — presumably Hamish — laughed. "Get yer bet on what day he comes round that corner as we go round the other?"

"Nah, he'd make it a different day on purpose. He would too," she added to Charlie. "A bit up himself is our Jacob. My twin and never forgiven me for popping out first."

"You said it," Hamish, who had overheard, replied. "Older sisters are the pits. Fair enough, save your money."

He turned away then high-fived a boy who came around the corner at the same time as a clapped-out single decker that seemed to jerk and judder as the engine spluttered as it jolted along.

The guy and the bus arrived at the stop in unison. The bus wheezed and stopped a few feet away from Charlie and Lily. The guy grinned and stopped even closer.

"Who's the bird?" His attitude was of someone full of themselves as he winked.

Lily's eyes narrowed. "Moron," she said under her breath. "My brother, as if you can't guess. Do I tell him?"

"Can do, or I can?" Charlie said a lot more confidently than she felt. To go up against someone who, she decided, was one of the 'in crowd' could backfire big time. But to ignore him could backfire even more. "Won't bother me."

Liar, liar, pants on fire.

Lily grinned. "Go for it."'

"Who's the gob," Charlie said sweetly, "who daren't ask me himself? Do you mean me, or is it that poor little, fluffy specimen on top of the bus shelter you were wondering about? That's a robin. I'm Charlie Allsop. You, I guess, are the bane of Lily's life."

The so-called bane stared at her for a second, narrowed his eyes then slowly grinned. "Gob, eh? Takes one to know one."

Charlie returned the long look-over he was giving her. She reckoned it was worth her time, even if he was a PITA.

I will not blush. Now she knew what it meant when she read about feeling dissected after someone looked at you.

Hot and bothered was an understatement, and she'd bet her next plane ticket to Hong Kong he knew it.

Jake Bannerman was one dangerous bloke.

He, meanwhile, didn't seem at all bothered by her scrutiny. Mind you, she was very careful which bits of him she scrutinized.

Tall, dark hair, gray eyes and a cocky grin. Stubble — designer, she guessed — graced his chin, and, oh for goodness sake, he had a dimple.

After several seconds, he raised his eyes from her boobs and nodded. "Sure does."

"Come on." Lily grabbed Charlie's arm and dragged her onto the bus. "I don't care if that lot think it's fashionable to be the last ones on, but one day… Argh… Got your bus pass?"

Charlie nodded. "Yep." She'd sorted it out a few days before. It reduced the cost to buy a monthly ticket, and as she still hadn't got round to buying a car, she guessed the bus pass would become her new best friend. She followed Lily onto the bus, not surprised to see her new friend sit next to the sole occupant. After all, she might be sociable and welcoming to a newbie, but she would have mates of her own.

Charlie showed her pass and went to a seat several rows behind Lily. She'd listen to music or check her emails or something.

Or look out of the window — it was only a ten-minute journey.

"Hi." The girl next to Lily twisted around, smiled and spoke to her. "I'm Mairi Sutherland."

"Darn it, sorry, Charlie," Lily said contritely. "Mairi, meet Charlie Allsop. Charlie, meet Mairi. She's doing English."

Mairi grinned. "Good to see you on here. Put the girls up to three from this stop then. Still outnumbered by morons, but hey-ho… Oh…" She glanced at Jake as he sauntered onto the bus. "Hi, Jake. Great to see you on here. You don't grace us with your presence often enough. I, er, we miss you."

Jake nodded. "Morning." He ignored the rest of her comments.

Mairi colored. "You going to the Rag Week meeting? They're wanting some new blood and ideas for different competitions this year."

Jake shook his head and Mairi's face fell. Someone, Charlie decided, needed to tell her not to show her feelings so obviously.

"Rugby," he said and turned to where Lily sat. "Hey, my seat."

Charlie looked up at Jake. His expression was one of…of what? A challenge?

She shrugged and did her best to ignore the way her heartbeat sped up. Not because he was hot — even though he was — but because here she was a newbie, challenging someone who she'd bet her new backpack was one of the leaders of the boys who ruled the roost. She'd no idea what they called them in that part of the world now, but before she'd done her year abroad, it had been the 'in crowd.' Something her gran always laughed about as she said it was a very sixties thing to say, but it fitted perfectly.

"Gonna move?" he asked.

Charlie stared at him. "No."

"I think you might." He loomed over her. "You see, my seat is where I sit."

"And I can't see anything that says this is your seat."

"Bannerman, sit down and let's go." The bus driver got into the act. "Can't set off until your ass is plonked down."

"You're holding the bus up," he said to Charlie. "The rule is bums on seats before we leave."

She raised one eyebrow. A new trick she'd practiced for ages. "Not me. My bum is where it's supposed to be. I'm sitting down, all ready to go."

Jake considered her and a wicked expression appeared on his face. "Okay then."

He swung around and sat on her. "Like I said, my seat."

He was heavy. Charlie made an effort to keep her face impassive.

"Like I said, not got your name on it." She shoved him. It was like pushing a brick wall.

Now what?

She decided the attitude to take was on the offensive.

"Ooft, who's been to the pie shop, then?" She dug him in the ribs, which were not covered in layers of fat, anything but. "Piggy-wiggy. At the risk of being personal, you weigh a ton and I don't want to be squashed. Move, you moron."

"Not unless you do." He shifted from side to side. "I could get used to it." He bent so his mouth was next to her ear. "Be better if it was you on top of me. Any which way. You fancy it?"

"Nope, I'm fastidious. No idea where you've been."

"You would then, though."

"Not interested."

He blew in her ear. *Asshole.* "Liar."

Hamish whistled and one of the other lads made stupid, suggestive noises.

"Jacob Bannerman, you're an idiot." Lily turned around and saw what was going on. "And I have to own up to the fact you're my brother. Thank god we don't look alike, or act alike. One idiot in the family is one too many. It's not your seat. You sit on the back row with your mates. Don't try to come it."

"Spoilsport." Jake stood up and bowed to Charlie. "I'll give you your seat. You're a bit too bony to be comfortable on." He turned to walk toward his mates as the driver put the brakes on and sighed audibly.

"You're a lot too arsy for me," Charlie retorted. What a twat.

To her surprise, he laughed. "Gonna have fun here. Your bones and my arse, eh? Could be good."

"In your dream," Charlie snapped, fed up of the way he'd decided to mock her. She couldn't help being rake thin, but with boobs. Her mum was the same.

Jake swung around and faced her. "Or nightmares."

He sauntered to the back of the bus and sat down next to his mates amid much laughter and backslapping.

What a twerp.

Chapter Two

He had to admit it, this new female interested him. Not that he'd show it, of course.

Jacob Bannerman wasn't known as Jake the rake for nothing. It had been earned by a devilish attitude and a way of making girls fancy him, before he showed them he wasn't interested. Not every girl—oh no, that would be tacky. He'd be the first to admit that he had stringent views on what he preferred in a partner. And that he lost interest very quickly.

Some might say that was once he'd got what he wanted, whatever that might be.

He rationalized it as so many females only one him. Or so he let on to anyone who was concerned.

Those who chased him didn't interest him. He liked to do his own chasing. However, Charlie Allsop was the first female in ages who appeared immune to his so-called charms, and it irked him. He was supposed to be the disinterested party, not the female.

Jake had no false modesty. He accepted that his looks were an act of nature—however, if girls fell for dark red almost burnished black hair and green eyes, who was he to ignore that? Or not take advantage? That would be foolish, and foolish was one thing he wasn't.

If older girls — women — came on to him, well, he wasn't going to *not* let them show him all *they* knew and *he* would enjoy.

Lydia Ffrench — with two 'f's — had made sure of that as an extra birthday present, one memorable evening in her dad's campervan. Jake had fond memories of Lydia. And the campervan.

Sadly they'd split soon after, but he'd put her tuition to good use when he could. Not as often as he'd like *or* as people imagined, but as he thought, enough not to feel as if his cock had shriveled up from lack of use. Pam and her sisters didn't get many outings there these days.

It might sound like a contradiction, but Jake was uneasily aware he could have sex and not really be involved.

What a shit I am. Maybe it was time to change his attitude.

However, old habits die hard. He whistled at a girl in his tutorial whose skirt could better be called a pelmet, and winked at Hamish who rolled his eyes.

"Not in your league, Jake."

"Nah, well below. But I can still admire her…legs."

First lecture over, he had a few hours spare and headed to the nearby golf driving range to hit a few balls. Golf wasn't his first love, rugby was, but he made enough money during the university holidays as a caddy to ensure he kept his eyes in.

As he lined up the ball thought about Charlie Allsop, and the thrill of the chase — and miss hit.

Concentrate. The next shot was better. Admitting his mind wasn't on golf, he wandered back into town.

Chasing Charlie. Nah, not my style. However, if he could get her to chase him, that would be different. Why, he pondered, did it matter so much to him that she showed no interest? There was plenty more girls in his lectures, or in the near vicinity, of a similar age – or older – who would go out with him without a second thought. That's why he chose to be a barman in one of the popular tourist pubs. No commitments and a lot of fun.

Jake, my boy, you're going to be a man slut if you're not careful. He pushed that thought out of his mind. Hadn't he just decided to turn over a new leaf?

Charlie Allsop… The look she'd furnished him with on the bus, the way she'd pushed back as hard as he'd shoved was not something he was used to. He wasn't sure whether he was amused or irritated by her and it. Or whether he would decide to teach her a lesson.

He and Lily chose to live at home, save money and, if they wanted privacy, use the bothy given to them as a retreat, borrow someone else's flat, or stop with whoever they wanted to be with. So far it had worked, but he realized if he got that far with Charlie Allsop, he had no idea if one of those options would be possible.

Ah well, a long way to go in that direction before, or if ever, I need to think about that.

Was it fate that meant his mum needed to borrow his car while hers was in the garage and so he'd used the bus? Otherwise he might not now be thinking about ways to get his revenge.

Jake was used to being the one who held all the cards. The one who dictated who did what, how and when. If he used his attitude to cover up the areas where he *was* unsure, he was confident no one knew that.

Charlie Allsop needed to know he couldn't be messed around with.

He was almost at the lecture hall when one of the lecturers, who he knew was in charge of the uni swimming squad, shouted to him.

"Hey, Jake, hold up."

He swore under his breath as he slowed his steps and waited, not very patiently, for the woman to reach him. He had no interest in swimming other than as a quick way to get some exercise and expand the number of sports he was good at.

"Not going into the team," he said before she had a chance to speak. "No time." *No inclination.* "I need to concentrate on passing my exams." True but not the reason, just one that he thought would resonate and be acceptable. "Need a good result to get a good job." *That* was true. He had his heart set on working for a charity that helped people via sport.

She tutted. "Pity. You'd be an asset."

Jake winked. Lucy Millen, the lecturer, was a friend of his parents and he'd known her since he was a kid in short trousers. "That's what they all say."

She laughed. "One day, Jacob, you'll meet someone who'll bring you down a peg or two. You know what they say about how the mighty fall."

"Ah, but you see, Mrs. Millen, I always bounce back up."

Unseen, a few yards away, Charlie heard the exchange. *What a PITA.* Having listened to Mairi when they were sitting side by side in the library, sighing over how she would have loved to have Jake sat on her knee and wasn't he hot, she wondered if her new friend was quite all there.

She gave him a blank look. "Hmm?"

Someone hissed at them to shut up, which meant she didn't have to stop herself saying hot wasn't in the repertoire of names she associated with Jake Bannerman. He reminded her of several guys she'd known when she was younger. Each and every one thought they were god's gift to females. Each and every one was, in her opinion, wrong.

A bloke had to have more about him than a pretty face, a hot-as-hell body and a sod-everyone attitude to be fanciable. For a brief moment she thought of Jean-Pierre, one of the guys she'd hung around with in Hong Kong. He'd had the good looks but not the arsy attitude. They'd had fun together but were happy to wave goodbye when she moved. She'd given him the new flippers he wanted, he'd given her a book of sonnets – in French – and a pair of earrings they'd seen in the silk market.

Somehow, she didn't think any relationship with Jake would end so smoothly, or in such a pleasant manner.

By lunchtime, Charlie's head was reeling. It was so weird to be back. So much seemed to have changed in the last year. Two new lecture halls built and one block of flats knocked down. The strangest thing seemed to be how many new people she'd met. Of course the people she'd been around before she did her year abroad were still there, but they'd moved in different directions. The friends she'd made and reconnected with in Hong Kong were still over there. She'd been the only person who had chosen to go from this uni to the one in Hong Kong.

She really felt like a fish out of water.

Charlie headed to the nearest café in a thoughtful and apprehensive mood. To be all alone after having such a large group of mates wasn't easy.

Grow up, buttercup. She was no wilting flower, and if she didn't make many friends it wasn't the end of the world, just a few months of her life.

Easier said than done.

People had been friendly enough, but she guessed they were waiting to see what she was like before deciding whether she was one of them or not. That was fair enough, but it didn't help her feeling of being a Billy-no-mates.

She looked around the crowded room and her heart sank. Not one empty table. Somehow, sitting down at a table where everyone seemed to know each other was a bit too daunting.

Resigned to eating her lunch standing up, she began to make her way across the room to where there were a few high benches.

"Hey, Charlie, over here."

She glanced around to see Lily's annoying brother wave to her from a crowd of boys sitting – or slouching – at a nearby table. Something in his expression made her wary. He hadn't exuded sweetness and light earlier so why now?

Probably because his expression was challenging.

Even so, she changed direction. If nothing else, it should show he couldn't intimidate her. Even if her knees were metaphorically knocking.

"Got to ask you, babe, weird accent, and all that. Where did you pop up from?" He tilted his chair back onto two legs and crossed one ankle over the knee of the other leg. For a brief, satisfying second, Charlie wondered if he would tilt too far…with or without a little help. Her foot itched.

"My mother's womb," she said laconically. "You?"

"Not from your mother's."

One of his mates sniggered.

"Now there's a mercy," Charlie said. "Because I don't want you as a brother."

"No?" He dropped his chair down and stood up, invading her personal space. "What do you want me for?" He leaned in close enough for her to smell his aftershave or whatever. Citrus and woodsy.

Damn him. Her mind went blank, and not one witty or semi-witty response was forthcoming.

"Nowt, I'm not into nightmares." Pathetic response, but the best she could come up with on the spur of the moment. She turned on her heel and walked blindly away, followed by laughter.

Bloody arsy, up himself...

"Charlie, there's a seat here." Lily dragged her down to sit next to her. "What's my moronic brother been up to now?"

"Trying to enjoy himself at my expense."

Lily nodded. "He fancies you."

Charlie shook her head. "Nope, he fancies himself."

Chapter Three

The month dragged on.

To Jake's relief his mum got her car back and, in turn, so did he, and took to driving to lectures again. Sometimes, if their schedules coincided, Lily begged a lift. Otherwise she chose the bus and her friends. He could understand the meeting up with friends bit, but not why anyone in their right minds was happy to sit on a deathtrap like a Duckworth's bus. He'd been lucky not to be leaning on the dodgy window that had fallen out — it was next to where he usually sat.

If he wasn't winding Charlie up.

Thank goodness that hadn't happened when anyone was using the vehicle. How the company dared to call themselves luxury coach travel specialists he had no idea. False advertising at its best. Okay, the next bus had been somewhat better, but even so. Driving himself meant an extra twenty minutes in bed each morning.

He walked out of a lecture one Thursday in a bitter mood. His lecturer had commented that if he took as much care over his essays as he did over the length of his hair, he'd be in line for a first class honors degree, but, as it was, he had no chance unless he pulled his socks up. Then, to top it all, rugby practice had been canceled due to a problem with the floodlights. David and Terry, his closest friends, were off doing milk round stuff—where various companies visited to see, as someone rudely put it, who they could poach from anyone else. The companies concerned weren't any Jake was interested in, and he was bored.

He drove out of the car park in a reflective mood.

What the hell was wrong with him? Apart from the lack of interesting female company. Introspection wasn't something he often indulged in.

However, he couldn't remember the last time he'd gone clubbing, had a stimulating conversation about anything other than sport or even got to first base with anyone.

Since Charlie Allsop appeared. Had she somehow put a hex on sex?

Life sucked. So did the weather. It was, as his gran would say, siling it down. Rain like stair rods, heavy and straight down.

Halfway home it didn't suck quite so much.

Parked—or stopped involuntarily—by the side of the road was a bus with a familiar logo on it, its hazard warning lights going twenty to the dozen.

Jake pulled in behind it, put *his* car's warning lights on and headed for the bus. As he approached the door, it swung open and Lily, Mairi and Charlie got out.

Lily spotted him first and waved. "Hi, guess what's happened."

"Run out of fuel again?"

"Not according to the driver." She rolled her eyes and pulled a funny face. "He says it's the gears. Sounded like lack of fuel to me, though. The two kids from the farm a few miles out rang their dad and he's bringing some green diesel. Illegal, but, as he said, needs must. I bet it will work."

The farm in question was up a long, rutted track and the children got on at the bus stop before the outskirts of town. Why it was up to them, and the driver just didn't contact the depot, Jake had no idea. Probably embarrassed.

"Don't bet on certainties." Jake looked at Charlie. "Bit of a change from your last commute?" Where had that been? He hadn't had a chance to quiz Lily, nonchalantly of course, about what she knew. He'd intended to do that later that evening.

Charlie grinned. "Just a bit."

"Private taxi?" He could just see that. She had the accent for it. Pan bread, as his gran would say. Posh Morningside, in Edinburgh.

She laughed. "Not exactly. Star Ferry across Hong Kong harbor. Along with dozens of others all in a hurry. Sardines had nothing on us sometimes."

Hong Kong? "You're from Hong Kong?" Why hadn't Lily told him that?

"After my mother's womb and a few other places, yeah. Someone's got to live there."

True enough, but somehow he hadn't thought of the fact she had. If he'd given it much thought at all, which he hadn't — okay, he admitted, which he *had* — he'd have thought the south of England.

"Bit of a change then, good old Duckworth's from a ferry."

She shrugged. "Both get you to where you're going. Allegedly."

"True. Okay, ladies, Jacob to the rescue. I'll get you to your next port of call, hop in." He nodded to his car. "No point in hanging around here."

Mairi's eyes lit up. "Thanks, Jake, I'll sit…"

"In the back with Lily," Jake said smoothly. "Charlie can sit in the front to direct me to her house." He didn't add, 'after I've dropped you and Lily off, and it doesn't matter whoever's house comes first.'

Mairi pouted. "But…"

"But do you want a lift or not?" Lily towed her toward the back seat of the car. "'Cause now's your chance."

"But I don't see…" Mairi said as she let Lily steer her toward the car.

"That's your problem, you never do."

Jake turned to Charlie with a wry grin. Lily had it right. "Ready? It's me, wait for goodness knows how long, or get wet."

"That's what we were going to do." Lily stopped and turned to Jake, still holding Mairi's arm. "Wait to see if it was fuel, then, if necessary, ring someone. We decided it's not really hiking weather in flatties," Lily said. "I thought you were going somewhere, though?"

"I am. Home. Rugby practice was canceled. No floodlights, someone must have forgotten to pay the electricity bill."

"Ha, well great for us they did. Come on, girls, let's get in or get soaked." She said something to Mairi in an undertone, as Mairi appeared to argue. Charlie stared after them and Jake bit back a snarky retort directed toward Mairi. Mairi wasn't going to be happy with her, and it wasn't her fault.

She must have realized because she sighed.

Would I rather get wet through and risk pneumonia out here – she nodded toward the car – *or be glared at in there?*

* * * *

143

Jake reached out and stroked a strand of hair from her cheek. His fingers were rough on her skin, but his touch was anything but. She shivered.

Attraction, go away. She had no intention of being the next Jacob Bannerman's whatever.

"So, Charlie, what's it to be? I'll keep you warm."

That was what she was afraid of. However, there was no real decision to make other than accept the offer. She didn't want to hang around, by herself for however long it took either to get the bus back on the road or for a substitute to arrive. It was almost dark, bloody cold as well as wet and if it didn't freeze soon, she was a monkey's uncle.

No monkeys in sight.

"I'll take the lift, thank you, but I'm happy to let Mairi sit in the front." Anything for a quiet life.

Jake raised one eyebrow. "You might be, I'm not."

That's me told.

Charlie settled herself and did her best to ignore the dark scowl she'd noticed on Mairi's face. Had no one ever thought to mention to her that blokes liked to think they were doing the chasing? That the saying a bloke chases a babe—horrible nickname—until *she* catches *him* was correct? If not, why not? Even she as a newbie could tell that Jake wasn't interested in Mairi, and that Mairi was upsetting only herself.

Not my business. She fastened her seat belt and waited until Jake got in and started the engine. "I live at—"

"Tell me once I've dropped these two off," he interrupted her. "Then we can talk."

The tone of his voice immediately made her wary. "About the state of the universe?"

"Nah, about us. You and me." He drove past the stationary bus with a toot on the horn and a wave to the driver. "Only you three left on?"

"Seems so. Lily said your mates were at a milk round day?" She wondered why he wasn't.

In spite of his attitude, and the fact she was sure he expected her interest in him, she *was* interested. Just not prepared to show it.

"They're still making up their minds what sort of job they're interested in." He shot a swift, speculative glance at her. "Bummed before uni, now scrambling for ideas. I almost did a gap year but decided I'd rather come straight here instead of traveling. Hey, I might have met you in Hong Kong. On the ferry."

"Stranger things have happened." Damn it, she was sure he noticed as she shot a swift glance at him and then stared out of the window. "I hate this weather."

"Yeah, it's shit. Now how about you? What did you do?"

"I didn't take a gap either."

He sighed dramatically. "Ha bloody ha. Trying to get information out of you is like trying to get blood out of a sodding stone."

"Lady of mystery, that's me." Charlie wriggled in her seat and laughed. She'd forgotten how much fun this needling in a nice way could be. Like this when he forgot to be up himself, Jake Bannerman was hot. Tingle-worthy. Someone she could go for in a big way.

"No stone to leave unturned or something." She considered her words. "And I have not a clue what I meant there so don't ask."

"Fair enough, I don't either. However, I do love a good mystery," Jake said in the sort of voice Charlie guessed he put to good use around susceptible females. Which she told herself firmly she was not.

"Why were you in Hong Kong?"

"What's this, twenty questions?" Why she didn't just come out and tell him, Charlie had no idea. After all, it wasn't a big secret. "Why not?"

He grinned. "Bet I won't need twenty. Question two coming up."

Out of the corner of her eye, Charlie saw Mairi lean forward and brace herself. She'd bet it wasn't going to be something non-confrontational. Thank goodness the rest of their friends and acquaintances didn't follow Mairi's attitude. The worst she'd heard from another Jake fan was, 'Ohh, tell me how well he kisses.'

Somewhat juvenile and, as she had no idea, it was easy to roll her eyes and say that instead of snapping, 'Grow up. If I knew, I wouldn't kiss and tell.'

"What was with the weird writing in your name?" Mairi asked Charlie. "I saw it when you filled your library form. Didn't make sense to me."

"That's par for the course," Lily said. "Not a lot makes sense to you, unless it's a chat-up line."

"That's horrid," Mairi said, and giggled. "But true. So?" she persisted. "What is it?"

"Snooping, Mairi?" Jake said in a sarcastic tone that made Charlie wince. "Those forms are supposed to be private and confidential, Mairi, and you know it. How would you like it if I said, ohh, Mairi, why do you have to have an inhaler, or a STD or something you really don't want other people to know about?"

"I don't have anything secret," Mairi retorted in a snippy voice. "Certainly not an STD, that's horrid.

"So's snooping and mega nosiness."

Mairi sniffed. "The form was on her desk, so I couldn't help but see as I walked past. If it's some great big secret she's only got to say."

"She is the cat's mother," Lily chimed in. "And rude. How would you like it if I called you she when you were there? Honestly, Mairi, what's got into you?"

"Nothing," Mairi said in a sulky voice. "I just wondered, that's all. Why are you all making such a big thing of it?"

"There's no secret," Charlie said sweetly although she wanted to curse Mairi and her nosiness. Was she like it with everyone or was it because Jake had been paying Charlie attention and not her? Probably the latter. She hadn't had the attitude at first.

It was stupid. Charlie had long decided Jake was being annoying only because she ignored his teasing. She didn't want it to upset or irritate Mari. She wanted to make friends, not enemies. "It's my name," she said swiftly. Anything to stop the sniping between friends. "My middle name, which is Mandarin. Not some weird writing script. Mandarin. As I said earlier, my mum and dad met in Hong Kong. I was born in the UK but they chose it for sentimentality. You pronounce it Shu Mai."

"That's pretty," Lily said. "What does it mean or is it a name like Lily or Mairi?"

Here it comes.

"It's Mandarin for little plum."

Chapter Four

Jake shot a swift glance at the young woman sat beside him and bit back the snarky retort he'd been about to make, mainly because he could tell she expected him to say something along the lines of plummy name, plummy accent, and it might be more fun to keep her guessing just when he'd comment — and how.

Commenting was of course what he had been about to do. Now he thought it much better not to and keep her wondering why he'd abstained.

"Pretty," he said. "My mum often says, if she'd given us middle names that meant anything, we'd be Jacob Poet and Lily Laval. She's convinced we were conceived in a tiny French village called Le Poet Laval when she and dad were on holiday." That was information he'd never shared before.

Lily laughed. "I'd've got the better deal there, I think. Can you imagine it? Instead we got our grandparents' names, George and Rose. What about you, Mairi?"

"Stevenson," Mairi said. "My mum's maiden name. Very traditional here." She didn't sound too happy.

What on earth was wrong with her? Jake accepted she fancied him, but he'd never shown her any encouragement. Not just because she was Lily's friend, but for the simple reason that *he* didn't fancy *her*.

"Then we'd have been Bannerman," Lily said. "As Mum was a Bannerman, no relation to Dad, before they married."

Jake laughed as he turned the corner toward the old house where Mairi's flat was situated. "Just as well they didn't follow tradition."

" You could drop me here," Charlie said. "It's not far."

"Nope, I'll take Mairi first."

"It would make more sense to leave me until last," Mairi said. "I don't mind."

He did.

"Nah, you, then Lily, then Charlie and then I'm off to the garage." He'd thought that up when he realized he wanted to have Charlie by himself for a few minutes. "Works better."

Charlie turned to glance at him. "How come if you don't know where I live?"

"Fate. Serendipity, Duckman's, means I'm being taxi driver. My internal sat nav says so." He pulled up outside Mairi's house. "Here you go."

* * * *

"So, little plum, where to?"

He'd dropped his sister at their home on the outskirts of town after a very disgruntled Mairi exited the car with a 'see you later' to Lily, a 'thank you so much, Jake' and what would have been a kiss on his lips if he hadn't seen it coming. He turned his head so she got his ear.

Lily had waved goodbye with a very over-the-top mimicry of the 'see you later, thank you, Jake' and a sloppy kiss. In the air, not on his body.

She giggled and he snorted. Charlie laughed.

"Sisters, who'd 'ave 'em." He turned the car around to face toward the village once more. "Thank goodness we love each other. You an only one?"

"Just me. I live along Hill Lane. Beech Cottage."

"You walk that in the dark? A bit different from Hong Kong and the Star Ferry. What about streetlights and things that jump out at you?" The road did have lights, true, but it wasn't the best-lit part of the town, even though Beech Cottage wasn't far along it. "Aren't you scared of ghosts? You must know the story of Poor Weeping Mary. She walks that lane every third Monday of the lunar month, weeping for her lost love and warning lone women to beware. Bet she'd listen to your little plummy self and think, here's one to talk to." What a load of crap he was spouting.

"As you say. God, you are an asshole, aren't you." Charlie didn't raise her voice. "Poor Lily, having to know she's your twin. You can love someone and not like them very much."

Her tone was scathing and if he hadn't been driving it would have made him squirm.

"Aww, you love me but don't like me? I can change your mind, honey plum."

"No need. I neither like nor love. I'll tolerate you 'cause I want a lift home and you're brother's mate. But I tell you, Jake, you are an idiot. Weeping Mary is more likely to say beware of blokes who think they're god's gift to women and in fact are god's curse. How the hell Mairi fan—" She broke off. "Sorry, uncalled for."

"I don't give her any encouragement," Jake said, annoyed he was now on the defensive. "I don't want to be brutal to her, she's Lily's mate, they were at school together. But while Lil and I stay at home and save money, Mairi chose to take a flat, to have freedom so she says. I don't intend that freedom to include me. She's getting almost stalkerish." He stopped the car outside Beech Cottage. "I don't fancy her, end of. She either can't or won't see that. Hamish does fancy her, and she ignores him. Go figure."

Charlie put her hand onto the door handle. He covered it with his.

"Any suggestions" — he leaned closer — "on what I should do?"

"Get a girlfriend, show her you're otherwise engaged."

"Good idea. Well, not the engaged bit, but the girlfriend bit. Are you volunteering for the post?"

If looks could kill, his mum would be choosing the hymns and he'd be pushing up daisies.

"In your dreams." Charlie unsnapped her seatbelt and got out of the car. "Thanks for the lift, and to set your mind at rest, I'm usually home a lot earlier than this so no, I'm not scared walking all of a hundred yards or so between streetlights."

Jake watched her saunter up the path to the door. He'd got an itch that said there might be a lot of Charlie Allsop in his dreams.

Damn the girl.

* * * *

Damn him. Not for a million pounds would Charlie admit that she hated walking up the lane in the dusk let alone the dark. She wasn't used to the silence or dense darkness between one pool of light and another. Noise and streetlights for her had always been plentiful, as had people. This lane with its scattering of houses was an alien land. One she hadn't got accustomed to. Hell, she was more familiar with the MTR — Hong Kong's efficient transport system — than Shanks' pony.

Okay it had been only a few weeks, but even so... What with the crappy bus and the dark nights, it wasn't an easy transition.

Suck it up. Some people have a lot worse commutes. She remembered another friend she'd made, Fiona, who lived on a farm a good mile from the next town where the bus dropped her off. As Fiona said, if her mum was busy, she just had to walk, whatever the weather, and roll on when she passed her driving test

At the door Charlie turned and waved. Jake might be an idiot, but he had brought her all the way home, so there was no need to be ungrateful. "Thanks," she shouted. "See you."

Jake got out of the car. "Hold on a sec." He jumped the gate — *show off* — and walked toward her.

"In the interests of harmony, and helping me and Mairi, do you fancy going to the cinema one night?"

It was the last thing she expected. Charlie gawped. "Say that again."

He scowled. "I wondered if you fancied going to the cinema, or for a pizza or something. We could try and not hate each other, and if Lily knew and told Mairi it might get her off my back. I mean she's a nice girl and all that, but not my sort. I don't want to embarrass her by telling her straight to back off, she doesn't deserve that. After all" — he winked and grinned — "I am fanciable, it seems."

And I'm just useful? Gee thanks. Not that she wanted him to fancy her but as a chat-up line it was lacking. "Pizza would be good. Sorry, but I, er, I hate the cinema."

"What?" Jake opened his eyes wide in astonishment put his hand over his heart and patted it. "You hate the cinema? No one hates the cinema."

"I do. It's too loud, it's too dark and it's either too hot or too cold. Plus I get bored."

Jake shook his head. "Bored? Watching a film? Strange woman. Not even go to see whoever your heartthrob of the moment is?"

"Nope. I wouldn't recognize whoever is in fashion if he jumped up and hit me on the nose." She grinned. "Who is in fashion?"

"Not a clue. I'm a bloke, I don't do fashion like that. Just new trainers or rugby boots. So, pizza. Tomorrow?"

Charlie considered him. It would be good to get out for an evening, he could be good company when he forgot to be the great 'I am,' and she did love pizza.

"Why not. What time?"

"I'll pick you up around seven." He bowed very theatrically. "Until the next time, little plum. Your parents should have called you Victoria."

Like I thought, asshole. He was going to make plum jokes forever more.

* * * *

News traveled fast. Charlie got onto the bus the next morning to see Lily grin and Mairi scowl. Maybe it was time to buy a bike.

"Only a moron wouldn't like the cinema," Mairi said in a voice designed to be heard by Charlie as she showed her pass and went to sit down. "I mean, really."

"Really," Charlie said. "I'm guessing you don't, then?"

Mairi gaped at her as Lily smothered a laugh.

"What did you say?" Mairi demanded.

Charlie was weary of it all. She hadn't even been out with Jake yet, and the nastiness had started. "I said each to their own. The world would be a very sad and boring place if we all liked the same things. Cinema isn't one of my pleasures. Luckily, I do like pizza."

"Well, it all seems a bit weird," Mairi muttered. "How do you know what's going on?"

"I read."

"Yes but..." Mairi appeared genuinely puzzled. "What about what's in and what's not? How do you keep up?"

"I guess I don't. Sorry, but that's life." Charlie went to sit down as her arm was tugged. She turned around to see Jake behind her. "Hi."

"Last-minute change of plan. Mum's got my car again, Dad's got hers." He stepped around Charlie and towed her down the aisle to a seat a few rows back from Lily and Mairi. "Let's sit here."

Charlie didn't have much option as he pushed her into the window seat and plonked down next to her. She waited until the bus set off then turned to him. "Why?"

"Why what, fruity plum?"

She supposed it could be worse. He might call her fruity loopy or plummy bum. "Why are we sitting here together?"

"Why not? I was going to suggest I drove you, and then Mum needed my car, so here I am. I'll have it back for tonight."

"Ah, good. There's no need to sit here, though. You can join your friends and I'll file my nails or something."

"My mum would say that's a 'here's your hat, don't let the doorknob hit you on the ass' sort of statement."

It *was* somewhat rude. "Yes, sorry, but there's no need to go OTT."

"You ain't seen OTT yet. That's for later." He settled in his seat sideways and spoke to Terry a few seats behind them, playing with an errant strand of Charlie's hair at the same time. She tugged. He held on.

"Let go," Charlie said under her breath. Really, he was too much. "You're hurting me."

Jake grinned. "No I'm not and I'm not letting go. I like playing with your hair. It's like silk."

She was going to be a gibbering wreck if he carried on like this. It was no good, she'd have to set some ground rules out.

Luckily, once they reached town, Jake left her with a swift peck on the cheek, a hug and a huge grin. "See you later, sweet plum."

Charlie smiled pseudo-sweetly. "Not if I see you first at this rate," she said under her breath as she headed toward the library. Lily caught up with her at the steps that led to the main door.

"Okay," Lily said. "Spill the beans. How long has this been going on? Why didn't you tell me? Mairi is spitting tacks, Mum's been threatened to get Jake's car back by six-thirty at the latest or else. When she asked why, Jake informed her, me—and Mairi who'd turned up after dinner—that he wasn't going to see the new blockbuster movie this week, as you don't like the movies and so the pair of you are off for a pizza instead." She raised her eyebrows. "I actually felt sorry for Mairi for about a second. She looked gutted. But then she started hinting she'd go with him, and how could anyone not want to go to the cinema, and I just got irritated. Jake didn't snarl at her, but I know him well enough to know how much of an effort that was."

"It's because of Mairi we're going. I guess I'm as good a smokescreen as any. He's trying to let her down gently. She's your friend, and he can't help but be around her, or her around him. I'm the sacrificial goat."

"Bleat, bleat. It's not that he fancies you, of course. Pull the other one."

Chapter Five

Of course he didn't fancy Charlie. It was a way out of a predicament, that was all, Jake decided as he pulled on new jeans and a favorite T-shirt. She was too young, too innocent…and too damned cute.

Not at all fanciable. *Ha, and if I could believe that, someone would have a bridge to sell me. Gullible dot com. Okay, I refuse to fancy her.* That was better—not. Who was he trying to kid?

However, he did fancy pizza and it was a way to solve the Mairi problem without too many tears. He hoped. Mairi was becoming ever more annoying and persistent, and he needed to be able to show her he wasn't interested without causing a stink. After all, she was his sister's mate. But meeting her on the landing when she was wearing a next-to-nothing nightie and then tripping accidentally on purpose so he had to catch her when she was having a girlie night with Lily was too much. Thank god he was still fully dressed when he saw the accident coming, and made sure he got hold of her at arm's length and not plastered to him as he supposed she aimed for.

Now if it had been Charlie… His cock responded to that like a wilting flower to rain.

Sadly, and sod it, rugby and getting a good degree came first, not a girl who set his senses reeling. He was having none of that.

If he was truly interested it would be different, but not only was she too close to home for comfort, he knew by past showing the moment he caught her he'd lose interest, and it could become awkward. Having once been out with someone who lived in the village, after they'd split up it had been difficult to act as if nothing had happened. Even if he'd fancied Mairi, that would have been a red, red, red, do not go there. She really *was* too close to home in more ways than one.

He would have to thank Charlie for helping him out.

An hour later, as they sat side by side in the pizza place, Jake had to admit that Charlie definitely wasn't that un-fanciable, however much he tried to think it. To his chagrin, she made it obvious she had no interest in him, except to do them both a favor. For, she said, it might annoy Mairi but would also help her not to be a Billy-no-mates.

"You've got Lily, Fiona and Amy and that lot," Jake pointed out. "Probably not Mairi but still, you have friends. Deffo not a b-n-m."

Charlie nodded. "Yeah, and to have attracted you will put a cachet on me. Make me more enviable and one of them. No idea why, though." She pulled a funny face.

It was obvious she was laughing at him. He couldn't decide whether to be annoyed or amused.

"I can't help being a catch." He rolled his eyes. "In the genes—that's g-e-n-e-s, not j-e-a-n-s, though…" He winked. "Who cares?"

"And modest with it?" Charlie crowed with laughter. "Come on, Jake, you're not known as Jake the rake for nothing. To be seen with you is something else. Or so I've been told ad nauseam. Almost put me off saying yes."

He wasn't sure how he felt about that. Or the fact Charlie wasn't bothered if she was there with him or not. "Why come then?"

She grinned. "I love pizza. I miss going out. That overruled being seen as your latest whatever or Mairi's sworn enemy. I'll have a Sloppy Giuseppe please. And dough balls to start with. Do they do Movember here? They used to have a Star Ferry with a mustache. Called it the Mo-Ferry. Cool. So?"

"Some do. Shall I?"

She shrugged. "All the same to me. What will everyone say?"

"Lily hates them and she says it's the only time a mustache is okay. Just for you I'll go for it if, you put some cash in the pot."

She laughed. "Ten pence, okay twenty."

"Cheapskate. What do you want to drink?"

"Fizzy water. And I'll check the puddings later." She put down the menu and passed him a fiver. "Mo-money. Oh and we're going Dutch."

"We are?" That wasn't something he was used to.

"Yeah you got us here, and presumably won't do a Duckworth's and run out of petrol." It had been confirmed that was indeed the case on the day Jake had rescued them. "Fair's fair, I pay half of the meal. After all, this is not a date, it's a helping out of the brother of a friend. A non-date."

Jake grinned and hit his forehead. "Bugger, that's snookered my plans for the way home. Turn the engine off surreptitiously, coast into one of the viewpoints and say 'oh dear, no petrol, what shall we do to pass the time.'"

Charlie giggled and he realized he'd not heard her sound so carefree before. He liked it.

"I'd say, 'why, let's play I spy and ring my dad,' of course."

"That's your idea of playing?"

She opened her eyes wide. "Well, duh."

"You plummy people have all the answers."

* * * *

They don't, of course, Charlie thought, as a couple of hours later they drove home, but they could give as good as they got.

The evening had been so much better than she'd originally thought possible. Once they'd got their initial awkwardness, and Jake's efforts to embarrass her, over, they began to relax. Jake accepted it was indeed a non-date, then they'd discovered they did have quite a lot in common. Both liked folk music and whom Jake described as the classic oldies. James Taylor, Carole King and The Rolling Stones. Both played the guitar, and admitted to singing a bit but not particularly well, or often.

"Comes of being bought up in a family of aged hippies on my part," Jake said with a grin after Charlie said she had no idea why she liked what she did. "My gran and grandpa actually went to Woodstock in the sixties and still rave about Joan Baez, Jimi Hendrix and mud baths," he continued. "Flower power at its best."

"I saw the film of it all," Charlie said. "It's one of the few things I've watched in a one-er, but I'll own up and say it was on a video. I've often wondered what it would have been like to be there."

"We've got that video, I spent hours trying to see if I could find my grandparents. Never did. Never did hear every last detail either but as Mum was born a scant nine months later, I think they indulged in the free love ethos with gusto. Still do. They live in a yurt, in France, where Lily and I go every summer and as Gran says 're-commune with nature.' And say enjoy life whilst you can." He slanted a glance at Charlie. "And you should always do as your grandparents say."

"So true. Mine said keep your legs shut and your arms folded."

The car swerved as Jake cracked up with laughter. "Is that a bit like wearing granny pants? That was my other gran's advice to Lily. She couldn't resist sharing it, especially as we know Granny France – to distinguish that Granny Bannerman from the one over here who is of course Granny Scotland, wears, as Lily calls them, scanties. And how the hell did we get on to discussing our grandparents' underwear?"

She had no idea, Charlie thought as Jake drew up outside her house – without any coasting, or stops in the viewpoint lay-bys. She wasn't totally sure if she should be happy or affronted by that. Not one tiny try-on.

"Thanks for the pizza and conversation." She unclicked the seatbelt with a snap that sounded like a bullet shot. "I hope it's helped."

Jake's grin showed in the dim light from the streetlight thirty yards or so away. For the first time Charlie saw he'd deliberately parked between two lights where the darkness was deepest.

"It helped. This should help even more." He unclicked his own seatbelt and leaned over. "So, lovely Charlie, can I say thank you for a very nice evening? For your excellent company and for anything else you think I need to thank you for?"

Charlie bit her lip. She could easily say, 'no don't worry,' get out and leave him as he was, or…

She went for the 'or,' and met him halfway.

His lips were soft on hers. His cologne, a citrusy woody number she didn't recognize, surrounded them. Then she lost coherent thought as that soft caress became harder and more enticing.

* * * *

Bloody hell. If anyone had asked, Jake would have emphatically denied a woman's response to his kiss could be so arousing. Especially on a first non-date.

"Wow, you're a…" Whatever he was going to say was forgotten as Charlie pushed at him furiously. He drew back before his gonads took over and he forgot where he was — outside her house — and whom he was with.

Someone he was sure wasn't ready to take it one step further. If he pressed her, she would have reason to hate him, and he didn't want that.

"A what?" she demanded. "What snarky comment are you going to come up with now? Rubbish kisser? Put out too fast and too soon? Not enough, too much, what?"

He stared at her in the dim light. Hadn't she enjoyed it as much as he had? "Eh? I bloody wasn't going to say any of that." He hadn't been, had he? "I was going to say thank you for a lovely evening, let's do it again."

Damn it, he could sense her blush.

"Charlie…"

"Do not say another word," she said in a fierce undertone. "I apologize, I was out of order. Thank you for a lovely evening as well." She got out of the car and darted up the path.

"Charlie, wait," he said in an urgent tone. "Let me explain."

She turned around and walked a few paces toward the car. Jake got out and rounded the vehicle to hold on to her arm. "I wasn't going to say anything horrible. Let's try it again. "He drew her closer and to his utter disgust, she was trembling. "Charlie, let me explain how you make me feel. Why I'm..."

He was what? Tongue tied?

"Finding it hard to tell you what I was going to say." Mainly because he had no idea.

"What is there to explain? We kissed, I thought you were going to say something negative and overreacted. I'm embarrassed at what I thought."

"Don't be. I could have thought that with some people I reckon. Not with you." He kissed her nose and she gave a small laugh.

"That tickles."

"One more thing I know about you. You're ticklish. Truce? I'll try not to sound as if I'm about to be a snarky sod, and you'll try not to react as if I am before I am?"

"I'll try, but you confuse me."

"That's okay, I confuse myself at times."

She did laugh then.

"So, next time our non-date ought to be a lift to uni tomorrow and maybe then the open mic night at the pub?" To participate in open mic night would be not only good fun, but show anyone who needed to know, that they were to all intents and purposes, a couple. What happened after was in the lap of the gods. *And her,* he thought.

"I guess. I don't want to put you out, though."

"You won't. I'll pick you up at twenty past, gives you an extra twenty minutes in bed." *Does she wear PJs or a nightie?*

Jake waited until she went indoors before he drove off, thinking furiously. What the hell was it about Charlotte 'little plum' Allsop that got to him?

Apart from great boobs.

Get your mind out of the boob scenario, Bannerman.

So much for his avowed, 'I'm not going to fancy anyone at school declaration.' That had gone out of his head well and truly when they kissed. All he could think of was *more*. And *where*.

Jake shook his head as he parked his car then headed indoors. He wasn't serious, it was all a means to an end.

So why was he already plotting where they could go next?

Chapter Six

"No Lily?" Charlie asked as Jake opened the car door for her the following morning. She wouldn't have blamed him if he'd sent a text saying he'd changed his mind. She'd spent a good two hours the night before wide awake, unable to sleep, reliving both his kiss and her stupidity. Two amazing things — in different ways and for very different reasons.

Then, when she had fallen asleep, she'd dreamed of him. Something new to her, dreaming of a bloke.

She'd woken up, sweaty and with emotions that, although not new to her, she'd never had the desire to act on before.

Arousal was a bugger when you couldn't — or didn't intend to — do anything about it.

She hated to admit it, but Jake Bannerman could become important. Not that she intended to let him know that. He would crow until the cows came home.

What was it with all these stupid animal and bird sayings? Raining cats and dogs — that had been Lily's comment the day before and Charlie had caught herself saying, 'Yeah, yeah, can't see any flying pigs around here.'

"Lily's opted for the bus." Jake waited until Charlie buckled up before he set the vehicle in motion. "With a little push from me."

"Is that fair?"

He shrugged. "Works well for our story. I'm taking you, she's going to do the 'thought I'd let them have half hour to themselves stuff.' Not that we can get up to much between here and uni and not be late for our first lectures. Pity."

"If you say so."

"Don't you agree?"

"I do actually, but hey-ho, that's life." *Shit, did I really admit that?*

Jake stalled the car.

"Another time, sweet plum?"

"Not if you keep calling me that."

"Shu Mai. I'll take you both home, though. We can drop Lil off first and take the long way to your house."

Charlie shook her head, somewhat regretful. "Not tonight, thanks. Mum's meeting me and we're off to town. Dad's birthday's coming up and we're going present hunting." How good it was to be able to say that. It was one thing helping him out, another to be thought of as always available.

Which was why, once they reached school, she got ready to get out with a cheery, "Thanks for the ride in. See you later."

Jake stopped her by holding on to her arm. "What's the hurry, babe?" It seemed, now they were outside the main lecture halls, the swagger was back in force. "We can go in together, I won't mind."

"Big of you. I might."

He laughed. "Come on, Charlie, remember what we're aiming for."

"You might know what we're aiming for. Me? I'm not so sure, apart from not being late to my lecture. Let go of my arm."

He did, and as she got out, so did he, and he faced her over the car roof. "We won't be late, we've beaten the bus. So let's finish this properly and go in together." He indicated toward where bus drew up, and where Duckman's was doing its usual juddering to a stop. "No point in getting this far and spoiling it all." He bent to get his backpack out of the car, locked the vehicle and walked around it to where Charlie still stood, undecided on what to do. With a wicked look that dared her to comment or make a scene, he put his arm over her shoulder and pulled her close before he took her bag and slung it over his shoulder with his. Together they began to walk toward her faculty building.

"You gonna cheer me on at rugby on Saturday? It's again New Thornhall and it's always a bloody grudge match. I mean bloody every which way. Be a good next step."

"If this backfires on me, Jake Bannerman, the good next step will be when I bloody your nose for you, never mind a rugby opponent," Charlie muttered as someone whistled and she saw the stricken look on Mairi's face. It made her feel awful. She wasn't out to hurt Mairi — just the opposite. "Mairi looks awful. Couldn't you merely have explained to her you weren't interested?"

"I tried that. It didn't work. She just ignored it and still gave out very heavy hints. I tell ya I felt stalked. Her 'oops I tripped' stunt on our landing when she was stopping over was the last straw. If Lily behaved like that

I'd've done my best to ground her for a year even now we're adults."

That made Charlie uncomfortable. "Really stalked or just always around and half of it could be coincidence?"

"Probably the latter, but hellfire, Charlie, I've known her since we all went to playgroup together. Hamish shoved a privet leaf up her nose, he tried to blame me and she said no it was him. I still maintain he did it 'cause he fancied her. Still does, for that matter, but because I said thank you, or as my mum said 'fank oo,' and kissed her, she's decided I'm the one. Hell, she even tried to get on the same degree course as me. Scary stuff."

It sounded worse than Charlie had imagined. "Yeah, okay, lead on, MacDuff."

Jake laughed. "Never call a Bannerman MacDuff. According to my dad's granddad, that's akin to heresy. God knows why, I've never found anything to substantiate it, and I love researching family history." He reddened. "And if you ever mention that, I'll tell everyone you're scared of heights."

"Oh so tempting, but as I am scared of heights... Okay, our secret."

"What is?" Mairi asked. She looked from one to the other. "What sort of secrets?" She and Lily had come close without Jake or her noticing.

"If we told you, it wouldn't be a secret," Jake said. "And none of your business."

Mairi looked as if he'd hit her. Charlie felt so sorry for the girl, but really she had brought it on herself. "Whether I'm prepared to eat tripe or not," she said hastily. "Jake thinks I hate it and I'm not telling."

Mairi appeared skeptical. "Hmm, if you say so. Would you eat it, Jake?"

He smiled. "That's a secret. Shit, look at the time. Better dash, ladies." He turned toward Charlie with devilment in his eyes, and bent and kissed her cheek. "Be good, babe. See you later."

Lily burst out laughing. "Oh my, he's got it bad." She glanced at Charlie and winked so briefly if Charlie hadn't been staring at her she wouldn't have noticed. "How about you" — she paused — "babe?"

"Definitely bad." Not that she intended to explain what was bad. Mainly as she had no idea.

Mairi harrumphed. "I'm going in."

Sadly that attitude set the tone for the day. The first three lectures, Charlie, Lily and Mairi were all in. Mairi ignored Charlie and at one point rudely talked over her. Hamish, Jake's friend and the guy whom Jake said fancied Mairi, collared Charlie as she left the union café later.

"What's got into Mairi? You going out with Jake?"

Charlie shrugged with an insouciance she didn't feel. "I don't know."

Hamish gave her a knowing look. "Fair enough, I do. Sod it, Charlie, the besom won't look in my way."

"Neither would I if you called me a besom. Rude, crude, lewd and bloody insulting."

"I didn't mean it like that," Hamish protested and reddened. "It's a wee besom sort of thing, a cheeky wee babe. A compliment."

"Ah, but if who you say it to didn't know that, they'd think you're talking about a woman of loose morals," Charlie said who'd discovered that meaning a few days before. "And not be best pleased."

Hamish went white. "Bloody hell."

Charlie nodded. "Just so. But, that apart, who knows what goes on in anyone's mind?" If she'd have been talking to another female she'd have added P.M.T. and rolled her eyes. As she wasn't, she didn't. "Can't help I'm afraid."

"Just go out with Jake. It's gotta help."

Charlie wasn't so sure.

* * * *

Halfway through the morning, she was even less sure.

She'd been asked by one of the lecturers—who also happened to be involved with the rugby teams—if she understood the rules of rugby. She did but unsure what agreeing meant she might be roped into said no. He'd sighed and nodded.

"Darn it. Oh well, I'm sure you'll learn if you go out with Jake for long."

That didn't sound very promising.

Nor did the three girls who said once Jake got what he wanted that was it, you were dumped.

"Usually by a text," one said. "Brutal but effective."

"But he's supposed to be very good at what he does," another said and peered closely at Charlie as if to divine just what he had done. "But then once he's dumped you…"

"You realize it wasn't to be, but it was fun while it lasted?" Charlie said sweetly. "And," she added as her temper got the better of her, "you know whether people are telling the truth or not and had fun finding out. Perhaps do marks out of ten for effort and originality and all that." She smiled because it was that or throw a strop. Sheesh, if one pizza brought on that sort of reaction, what would an evening in a darkened cinema do? At least she'd be spared that.

The first girl giggled. "Ten in everything," she said and sighed. "Even the text dumping."

"How long did you go out with him?" Charlie asked, interested in spite of herself.

"I haven't, I just hear things. You're the latest and there's bets being taken on how long it'll last. First date doesn't count, 'cause that could just be you being nosy. You're not his usual type." She did a big 'pity' sigh. "Except for the boobs. We all know he's a boob man."

Charlie glanced at the curvaceous girl in front of her and forbade to state the obvious, albeit bitchy, retort that sprung to her mind. As in, *well it must be more than just boobs if he hasn't taken you out.*

When Jake found her at lunchtime and did his "hello, my little plum" thing, she was ready to kick him.

"You," she said, "have given me a reputation already. And it doesn't sound that brilliant. Evidently first dates don't count, who knows why you chose to go out with me except for my boobs, and how much will I put out and when. Charming."

To her chagrin, Jake laughed. "Ouch, poor yummy plummy."

"You can say that again. Bye." She spun on her heels and went to march off. It was that or hit him.

He stopped her by taking her hand. "Sorry, Charlie, but seriously, you've got to laugh."

She did?

"So you say, but I hate it. What's so great about you anyway?" she asked half-seriously as she turned to face him. "Apart from genes."

"I'm great in bed." He waited for a second and winked. "Allegedly. Wanna find out if you agree?"

What the hell did he sound like? Charlie gaped at him, and realized by his expression Jake went to backpedal fast.

He was too late.

"Asshole." She slapped his face and pushed him so he was unbalanced enough for her to drag her arm away, annoyed that actually, yes, she did want to discover if she agreed or not. "I was right, you're not worth spending time with." She walked off.

"You're magnificent when you're angry," he called after her. "Shall we have sex now or later?"

She flipped him the bird.

Chapter Seven

Charlie could only be glad her mum picked her up and they drove into Edinburgh to do some early Christmas shopping as well as presents for her dad's birthday. The Christmas market was being built, but sadly not in operation. Charlie wondered who she could persuade to go with her later on.

Jake? More likely to be Lily.

"What about something for Jake?" her mum said with a twinkle in her eye. "You seemed quite, er, enthusiastic about your night out."

"Huh, I like pizza. Him I reserve judgment on."

"Don't cut your nose off, love. He's a bloke. By definition all blokes are arsy, up-themselves idiots at your age and some never grow out of it. Think of your Uncle Arthur."

Charlie sniggered. Her mum's brother was such a good example of that sort of male.

"You just have to overlook that and delve deeper," her mum went on. "More often than not it's because they really aren't confident or sure of themselves. Most of them are a heap of insecurities, and it's their way of covering that up."

Her mum laughed, but she set Charlie thinking. Was that the way it was with Jake? It could well be.

She chose a T-shirt in a shop she knew—from Lily's chatter—he liked, and thought that if they weren't on better terms by Christmas she'd keep it or put it into the Presents for People Charity box.

They drove home after a successful present-buying session. A retro radio for her dad as well as a new sweatshirt and some of his favorite licorice sweets, and some stocking fillers for each other. Bought in private, of course. When her mum wasn't around, Charlie nipped into the chemist and bought some condoms. Better to be safe than sorry. She really ought to make an appointment with the doctor to go on the pill. Charlie was under no illusions. She was going to have sex with Jake sooner or later and intended to be prepared. She got some deodorant for herself and some scent Lily had said was her favorite as well, just in case her mum noticed what shop she came out of.

Her phone signaled a message just as they finished dinner. A text saying 'lots of love and sorries from the asshole. Pick you and Lil up after lectures tomorrow? I'm not going in until lunchtime, so you'll have to put up with the bus in the morning.'

She thought about it. He could wait. It wasn't until she got into bed she answered him.

With a thumbs-up emoji.

* * * *

The ride to town the next day was horrendous. It was cold, the heater on the creaking old bus didn't work and Charlie wondered how in hell it passed all the tests needed to keep it on the road. To make matters worse, Mairi was downright hostile and kept up a continuous stream of snide comments.

In the end, Lily told her forcefully to shut the hell up. "Look, Mairi, he doesn't fancy you, never has fancied you and bloody well never will. Get over it. It's not Charlie's fault, if she wasn't here he still wouldn't fancy you. And yes, that is harsh but true. I hate to see you like this. Snap out of it. Build a bridge and get over him."

Mairi gasped, firmed her lips and moved from her seat next to Lily into a vacant one. Lily shrugged and turned to Charlie who was a few rows behind as per usual. *Had to be said*, she mouthed.

As they got off the bus, Mairi pushed past them and headed off to the library. Lily sighed.

"We've been friends for ages and until she got this fixation about Jake she was fine. Always a bit intense over certain things, but not like this. I told him he'd have to be cruel to be kind, but he was adamant he couldn't do that, she was my mate. Well, he was spitting tacks the other day at her antics and now the way she was with you. One step too far. Are you okay?"

Charlie nodded. "Sticks and stones." She thought over what Mairi had said. "I have no idea how good he is in bed." Or out of it, for that matter. As far as Charlie was concerned, a kiss was nowhere enough to decide such important things.

"Nor has she, and that's what pisses her off. There's plenty of women around who happily say he's the best." She rolled her eyes. "Though if they'd all been to bed with him, he'd have no energy for rugby."

Charlie laughed. "If I ever get to find out, do you want me to give you his marks out of ten?" she asked mischievously. "One score for stamina and one for artistic effort?" She winked. "And you can do the same about Terry."

Lily blushed and chuckled. "You sod. Ten and ten and there's a bothy on our land that's only known to our family. Decked out as a retreat for Jake and me. We tell each other if we want to use it. And before you say anything else, he's never taken anyone there." She paused. "Wonder if that is about to change? I won't be needing it this next week. Terry's off to see about doing a post-grad degree at Edinburgh. Shall I mention that to him?"

It was Charlie's turn to redden. "Don't you dare." She had no intention of mentioning she had her own house. Not yet.

* * * *

True to her word and to Jake's surprise, Charlie and Lily were waiting by his car when he came out of the Humanities building five minutes late and at a run.

"Sorry, got caught by Bloody Slimy Sturgeon who is still going on about an essay he says I didn't hand in and I say I did. It was put in his pigeonhole. I bet he picked it up and just put it down somewhere. Honestly he was awful as a teacher, but now he's transitioned to a lecturer he's ten times worse." He'd been a teacher at their old school and had never approved of Jake since Jake had burned a hole in the science lab desk when he first started at the school many years earlier.

"I told him I was going for Movember and it was the start of my mustache. He gobbled a bit, but couldn't really say anything anyway as Mrs. Macklin walked by and winked and told me she was glad I was participating and hoped I'd make a lot of money for charity." He sighed dramatically. "She's a bit of all right."

"You just like her short skirts and thigh-high boots," Lily observed. "Blokes and their gonads."

Jake laughed. "Not just those. She has good…outlines as well."

Charlie sniggered. "Must remember that one."

Jake shrugged as he unlocked the car. "I was being polite. Yours are outstanding."

"'Bout time you were polite," Lily said as she got into the back seat, unasked. "You forget a lot."

"Nope, just can't be arsed, unless the situation warrants it." He shut Lily's car door and opened the front passenger seat for Charlie. "Like now. Okay?" he asked as she got in and tucked her bag under her legs. "Comfy?"

She nodded. "Thank you."

He bowed. "You're welcome."

The atmosphere in the car with no Mairi about was so pleasant, Jake didn't even mind his sister was there. They had very few secrets from each other. She knew when he had first had sex and he knew when, in her words, she'd popped her cherry and he was told in no uncertain terms not to pop Terry's nose.

"Consensual," she'd said. "Bloody good."

As he'd thought he himself could do better than on his first time, he kept his mouth shut.

It was getting foggy as they drove down the road and over the area called 'the bumps.'

"This reminds me of that place near where my gran used to live in the Trossachs," Charlie said. "This weather gives me the creeps. The land around her house is fairly boggy, adjacent to a proper bog called The Moss, and the road always begins to sink and become uneven over the years. When the fogs and mists roll in it can be eerie. When he was younger, before he had passed his car driving test, my dad rode a moped and hated driving down that stretch in the dusk, mist or dark. The bumps made his headlights flicker, he swore you saw ghostly figures and heard eerie noises, and said he was damned glad when he passed his driving test and got a car."

Charlie shivered. "So now you know why this weather gives me the willies."

Jake choked.

Charlie rolled her eyes. "Trust you. Toilet humor."

He nodded as they drove around a sharp corner and toward his home.

"Trite but true. But yeah, it gives me the shivers as well, and not the sort I get when I touch you," he added softly, even though Lily had headphones on and was nodding in time to whatever she was listening to. "Or what I know I'll get when I do touch you."

"Yeah?" She glanced sideways at him. "I'll keep that in mind."

"How long for?"

She gave him the sort of considering look that made his cock perk up and demand to be noticed. He did his best to ignore the fact his trousers were now considerably tighter.

"Well…when's your bothy empty?"

Thank God they'd stopped outside his house to let Lily out. He'd have stalled the car again for sure if they hadn't. His heart missed a beat and sped up. "I don't know but I'll be damned sure to find out."

As he put the car in gear and drove toward Charlie's house, Charlie smiled like a cat that had got the cream.

"I do. Lily doesn't want it this coming week. How about tomorrow? I don't need to be up early on Saturday. What time's your rugby match?'

"Three, so nor do I." His heard beat slowed to normal-ish. Sod the no sex before a match rule. Surely sated was better than frustrated? "Er, are you still up for open mic night tonight? We won't be later than ten home."

"Sure. I can make that half past ten. I'm up to date with my studying."

"So am I. That gives us time to neck."

"One track mind. It gives us time to sing." She grinned. "And neck."

Thank goodness.

"Will you be happy to walk? Then we can both have a drink." He paused. "Just one or two."

"Well, duh. It's not that far for me, but how about you?"

"I'll suffer or get a cab. Pick you up at seven?"

And make sure the bothy was all ready for the following night, and buy some more condoms — just to be on the safe side. Tomorrow, he'd pop out at lunchtime — luckily the nearest supermarket was only twenty minutes from where he had his last lecture of the morning, so as long as he ate 'on the hoof', he'd have time to get there and back and not be late for the afternoon tutorial.

Would it be tacky to sing, 'we'll have the time of our lives,' to alter that famous title a bit?

* * * *

"I so enjoyed that," Charlie said as they walked back up the road, hand in hand, several hours later. "I reckon we brought the house down with 'The night they drove old Dixie down.'"

Jake laughed. "Not to mention cabaret and your high kicks."

Charlie bit her lip. "I got carried away a tad there. Sorry. I blame my glass of wine."

"Don't be, you're the envy of the dancercise class now. And one glass of sauv blanc does not a dancer make. Or sommat."

"True, ah well, I enjoyed it."

Jake grinned. "So did most of the pub."

"Oh grief, did I really show myself up? Show us up?" Charlie giggled. "Can I show my face again?"

He hugged her. "Yes you can, and no you did not. You are now a fully paid-up member of the karaoke society."

That sounded okay to her—maybe. "That's good then." They were almost at her house. Charlie stopped walking and turned to him. "I have to ask... If we"—she mimed quote marks—"if we do the deed, what then?"

"How do you mean?"

"Will it be okay, thanks, bye, end of? A Dear Joan text. Glad to have had you, don't want you anymore crap? Because if that's the way you play, the game is over. We might not last long, but I'm not having sex when it's sex and end of." She peered at him in the faint light of the nearest streetlight. "Sorry if that offends you."

"It does. What do you take me for?"

Charlie rolled he eyes. "Come on, Jake, I've heard the stories ad nauseam. Jake the rake. Jake the text sender. One strike is enough. I deserve more than that."

Shit, he looks really hurt. She rushed to make amends. "At least two strikes please. Pretty please with bells on." Charlie went onto tiptoe to kiss his cheek. "Jake, I like you, really like you, or I wouldn't be getting ready to have sex with you. But we deserve more than one roll on the bed or whatever. So…" She let her voice trail off and crossed her eyes. "At least two rolls?"

He was so quiet Charlie wondered if she'd stopped everything before it started.

At last he sighed. "I guess I deserved that. Okay, at least two."

Thank god she'd got that doctor's appointment the next morning.

Chapter Eight

"This is fabulous," Charlie said the following night as she looked around the tidy, tiny cabin with interest. It was warm and toasty, due to a plug-in heater. Jake had told her there was electricity run from the house into it, plus Wi-Fi. "Isn't it great to have somewhere to call your own?"

Jake nodded. "Even if I do share it with Lily. We've worked out a system so we don't tread on each other's toes." He winked. "Or pinch each other's condoms and not replace them."

She took a deep breath. "If she needs it, we can use my place. It's mine, all mine, at the moment." She chose not to mention it had been all the time.

"Say what?"

"It's my house. Oh, and in the interests of full disclosure and all that, I went to the doctor's to get a prescription to go on the pill, but don't get happy-clappy. Won't be useful for at least a month. So…" She gave him what her mum called 'the look.' "I got condoms as well."

"So did I, but thank you for the pill bit. Double protection and all that."

She slanted him a sideways glance. "Ah, but will you benefit for it?"

"What? I bloody better."

Charlie laughed at the astonished look on his face. "We'll see. You might be sick of me by then or me of you."

"Nah, we need to learn together, babe."

Charlie punched up a pillow on the settee. Lily had told her if you took the back cushions off it was just about the size of a single bed. More than a few of people had done just that, she guessed.

Jake nodded toward a small fridge in the corner of the rom. "Drink?"

"Water. I want to keep my wits about me." She had a feeling she needed to.

"Pity, I was going to hold on to them for you." Jake took out two bottles of water and passed one to her. "I'll keep the fizz for later."

She nodded and began to wander around the room. Probably the size of her bedroom at home, it was kitted out like a bedsit, with the settee, a tiny dining table and two chairs and a shelf with a kettle and a microwave.

"Do you ever stay overnight?"

Jake nodded. "Lily and I both have. There's bedding under the settee, which can open up as a double bed as well as working as a single. It's better than a tent. Warmer and a hell of a lot more comfortable. I've never brought anyone here before overnight. Just let me know if you want to."

"Well, as we don't have to hurry."

"That's a lovely thought." He almost purred the words. "I'll make it up now."

Shit. His voice was doing strange things to her body. Whoever would have thought a tone could make your toes curl in anticipation? "How about we start lesson one?" he added as he played with her hair.

"What a good idea."

Shit, was that really her being so forward? She could hardly believe it as she watched him swiftly change the sofa into a bed. Nor could she grasp how the act of Jake then putting her on his lap and undoing her blouse buttons one by one could make her nipples hard and her clit throb.

As for the tingle that hit her with a regular beat…

Oh my, the tingles.

Jake smiled. Was there a bit of self-praise in his expression? Complacency or a 'ha, knew she'd give in to my charm sooner or later?' "Ready to discover the road to ecstasy?"

For some unfathomable reason, his confident attitude irked Charlie. He was oh so certain he was the one to show her everything. He slipped her blouse from her and made short shrift of unhooking her bra and slinging them onto a chair.

"Oh my, what have we here. Whatever you've heard about me being a boob bloke, it's true. I love a good pair of tits and yours are the best."

Crude bugger.

"I like a good cock, let's hope yours measures up."

Jake's draw dropped, then to her surprise and pleasure, he broke into a loud guffaw. "Touché, love."

He bent his head and laved each nipple in turn. Her annoyance vanished as they responded by tightening and *that* tingle became a sweet pain that hit her in the best possible way. Charlie's thighs were damp, as Jake laughed softly and blew on each rock-hard nub.

He's done that more than a few times. Sod it, enough already. I wouldn't want him to not know what he was doing.

"I'm so looking forward to showing you everything," Jake added as he pulled his T-shirt over his head. "Thank you for coming and letting me."

"You won't be my first," Charlie said.

His astonished, disappointed expression made her wish she could rescind the words.

"No?"

She shook her head. "No."

Damn, she saw how that shook him. He carried her to the sofa bed, put her down as if she were precious porcelain and stripped as he looked at her. He finished undressing her and began to stroke her until she was wet and panting. Then he moved so his cock was just touching her cunt.

"Ah well, I'll just have to be the best."

He pushed in firmly. Stopped as she tensed.

"More," Charlie said firmly. "Don't stop, give me more."

The pain was short, sharp and oh so welcome as he thrust firmly until he was deep inside her, waited for a second then began to move.

He was large, hard, hot and it was heaven. She began to move in time with him.

"Won't last long," Jake gasped.

"Don't w…w…o…r…r…r…ry, nor will I."

"Then we better make the most of every second." He withdrew and bent his head to nip her clit then laved her labia.

Charlie arched upward, not sure if it was to ask for more or to beg for release. His tongue on her skin was rough but tender, hot but soothingly cool, exciting, erotic, arousing and…and…she ran out of coherent thought as he used it to delicately probed her channel.

His cock might not be in her, and although the sensations were different, they were no less exciting. She keened. A sound she had never heard herself utter.

He lifted his head and mouth and laughed. "Oh yes, we both like that."

"Understatement, damn you." How she spoke coherently, Charlie hadn't got a clue. "More, I need you in me."

"Soon." He blew softly on her clit.

"Now." Damn, was that her needy begging voice she could hear? "P…l…e…a…s…e…oh, please."

"Soon." He licked her once more then moved to pinch her nipple between his taut lips.

"Nooo… Now…"

He laughed. "Okay, now."

Before she'd drawn breath he filled her. Each movement triggered a ripple of sensation inside her. The deeper he plunged, the harder her reaction.

He paused, his cock only just inside her, before he once more moved smoothly to fill her. Charlie got the familiar, it's now stings and shards of pleasure-pain over her skin. Goosepimples covered her and she shivered in anticipation.

Jake thrust hard and fast. She splintered.

Her screams mingled with his shouts as she let herself go and plunged into the vortex of ecstasy and an orgasm.

By the way he shook, it was a foregone conclusion that he'd followed her to that secret place where no one and nothing could interfere with that amazing pleasure and state of sated satisfaction.

* * * *

"You lied," he said flatly. "I was your first." He ran one hand down her body in a proprietorial manner as they stretched out together, legs entwined, hot, sweaty and sated. He'd got rid of the condom in the tiny bathroom, and returned to the bed with a bottle of champagne and two glasses.

"I didn't say first at what," Charlie said as she savored the last hour in her mind. "At least you know you're the best." She chuckled. "For now."

"Ha." Jake grinned and held his glass of fizz above her body. "Forever. You know? I've always wanted to do this." He tilted his glass so the wine reached the rim.

"Don't you dare. Argh, you sod... It's cold."

He'd dared, and cold fizzy champagne dribbled onto her stomach to pool in her navel.

"Now, of course I'd better dry you." He put down the glass and lapped at the wine.

Charlie squirmed. "That tickles."

Jake lifted his head. "Then hopefully this won't." He moved his mouth lower and delicately licked her clit.

Charlie arched up off the bed. "Ohhhh, m...y..."

He lifted his head and licked his lips. "Is that a good, 'oh my'?"

"The best."

"Then..." He dipped his head again and this time tongued the entrance of her channel before he pushed inside.

Charlie gave up thinking as he proceeded to lick and lave her to another climax. She screamed and he moved to cover her mouth with his.

For the first time, she tasted herself.

Salty, musky...not unpleasant, she decided as she floated down from the ceiling.

"You didn't come," she said as her brain unscrambled.

"Will do in a sec, if you're not too sore."

"Sore? Nah, I'm invigorated," Charlie said and crossed her eyes.

Jake laughed as he put a condom on with shaky hands. "I've unleashed a monster."

"Yeah, great, isn't it? You know I would love to do that." She pointed to his condom-sheathed cock.

"Next time. I wouldn't have got past you touching me and not come this time. I want to come inside you.

"Then I'm all yours."

She meant it.

* * * *

She still meant it three weeks later when Mairi cornered her in the union cafeteria doorway. "Going to the Uni Christmas Ball?"

Charlie shrugged. "No idea." Jake hadn't mentioned it so she hadn't brought it up. They had carried on seeing each other, had two more long, hot and incredibly amazing sessions in the bothy as well as a trip to the local town for a curry, and another so she could help him buy a Christmas present for Lily, talked about anything and everything, but the ball hadn't been a topic.

Mairi smiled maliciously. "Jake never takes anyone." She shrugged in a very over-the-top way. "He says he *will* but… The number of girls who think he'll meet them there and then he ignores them…" She rolled her eyes. "They might have been going out with him but come the dance… More fool them *for* going out with him."

"As you say. Has he never asked you then?"

Mairi scowled. "I wouldn't say yes."

"Then you've nothing to worry about, have you?" Charlie looked Mairi in the eyes. "Bless you." She walked around her and into the café where Jake waved to her and indicated the seat next to him.

"What's up? You look ready to spit nails."

She sat down, tucked her legs under the table and ignored his hand on her thigh. "And in Mairi's direction. She's just informed me if you suggest to someone you'll partner them to the ball you'll stand them up. Charming."

He reddened. "I never actually ask anyone. I always try to go by myself."

"Then let's not let this year be any different, eh? Yes, I know you haven't asked me either, and I wouldn't presume." Even if she had, torture wouldn't get *that* out of her. "So now you don't need to get your boxers in a twist over what to do."

If she weren't so angry, his look of astonishment would have made her laugh.

"Charlie, I…"

"Don't worry, Jake, I'm not." *Liar.* "Are we still okay for open mic tonight?"

It was evident her easy acceptance of him and the ball, which was one of the biggest entertainments of the semester, puzzled him.

Good. It infuriated her.

"Er, yeah, if you fancy it?"

"Of course I do. We have so much fun." She stood up and kissed his ear then whispered, "Don't worry, I won't stand you up."

Jake grinned. "You can't. I'll come for you."

"I could be out." She paused. "But I won't."

* * * *

"What are you wearing for the ball on Friday?" Lily asked as she and Charlie walked into town one lunchtime for a mooch around the few shops and to get some chips and cheese instead of the usual cafeteria offerings. Chips and cheese were something Charlie had never tried until she moved to Scotland, but she was now a fan. The local chippy put slices of what Lily described as 'cheap and plastic' cheese over piping hot chips so it melted and went all gooey. She and Lily had taken to having it as a midweek treat. Mairi, still in a snit, didn't go with them.

"I've got this cool hippy dress because this year's theme is the '60s," Lily continued. "I'm guessing most people will be in miniskirts so I thought I'd be different."

"Not sure I'm going," Charlie said as she dipped the end of one cheesy chip into the tiny pot of tomato sauce she'd chosen. "Sounds like you'll be the best of the best."

"And why do you think you're not going?" Lily narrowed her eyes and scowled. "Who's said what?"

Charlie shrugged.

"Fess up, woman. You can't tell me you and Jake have finished because I was the one who lost the toss of the coin for the bothy tonight, seeing as the ball is on Friday. He doesn't want the bothy to revise and remind himself of what he should know. Unless, of course, he wants to remind himself of your curves."

Charlie sniggered and coughed as her chip got stuck in her throat. Lily patted her on the back and shoved a bottle of water into her hand. "Drink."

Charlie drank and wiped the tears her coughing fit had brought on. "Between you and me, Jake hasn't asked me and I told him not to bother. I've been told by several people, some in a nice way and some not, that he never takes anyone to any uni activities. Though he has been known to disappear during some of them for a while with whoever took his fancy. Who, someone took great delight in telling me, might not be with whom he'd been going out. Such a charming attitude. So I told him not to worry about the ball and were we still going to the open mic night the next night. We did and as you say have enjoyed ourselves rather a bit since then." She rolled her eyes. "Okay, a lot. But as for the bop on Friday, well…"

"Well, you're going, you've got to, it's the last big do before we sit our next exams. Come with me and Terry."

"Nope, I'm not green and gooseberry-like. I refuse to be the unwanted third."

"Rubbish, it's not like that. In fact…" Lily's eyes gleamed. "Can I play devil's advocate?"

"You can, but why?"

"Because my brother is an ass. Do you trust me?"

Charlie laughed. "With reservations." She'd leaned to be wary of Lily and her bright ideas. "What have you in mind?"

Lily shook her head and put a cheese-covered finger over her lips. "Sealed," she said once she'd moved the digit. "Wait and see. Just hunt out your miniskirt or whatever. I'll sort your ticket."

Chapter Nine

"You and Charlie going to the ball tomorrow?" Lily asked casually as she passed Jake on his way home from a breathtaking, hot, erotic evening with Charlie. He couldn't get enough of her. Never before had he, Jacob George Bannerman, felt like this over anyone. It was both fantastic and frightening.

He stopped midstride. "Why?" he asked suspiciously. "I never take anyone to any uni dos. You know that."

Lily shrugged. "Just wondered."

"Who's been saying what, Lil?" Jake demanded. First Charlie, now Lily mentioning the damned ball. He was in two minds whether to go or not. Even so, no one, but no one, would force him into changing habits of a lifetime and taking a girl. Even if he did consider that Charlie was his girlfriend, and had no intention of going out with anyone else. "Who's the stirring shitbag?"

"No one as far as I know. I just wondered, that was all."

"Then wonder no more. We're not going to the ball together."

"Ah, thanks for letting me know."

"Lily, what are you up to?"

"Me?" She opened her eyes wide. "Not a thing. I just know Marcus fancies her and if you're not taking her…"

"If he does, it will be the last thing he does with a full set of teeth."

Lily laughed. "I'll tell him." She disappeared upstairs before he had a chance to say anything else.

Jake followed her slowly. Charlie wouldn't go with anyone else, surely. But then, he reasoned, *If I'm not taking her, why shouldn't she?*

That didn't sit well.

He drove both Lily and Charlie home the following evening, and, as ever, Lily got out first.

When they got to Charlie's house, she leaned over for a kiss, which he gave her. Then she straightened. "Enjoy the bop. See you at rugby tomorrow."

She slid out of the car, waved and walked up to her front door.

Jake stared after her. Just like that? No recriminations, no questions, nothing.

Does she not care?

He wasn't in the best frame of mind as he drove home and got ready for the evening ahead. He hadn't had a chance to mention it to her, to see if she was going or not.

Bannerman, you are a bastard. How can you expect her to be sanguine about it all, whatever she says? And what sort of a shitebag am I if I go to the ball and chat up someone else? He rang Charlie.

She answered her phone and he could hear the cheerful burble of the TV behind her. "Hi," she said cheerfully. "What's up?"

How to answer that.

"I, er, I wondered if you want a lift to the ball," he gabbled. "You never said how you were getting there."

"Ah, no, it's fine, thanks. Have you decided what you're wearing? Lily said Terry has a fabulous pair of flares. He's going as a hippy, of course."

Jake was speechless. Didn't she care they weren't going together? She'd never mentioned the entertainment of the evening apart from telling him not to worry about her. "I've got my granddad's winklepicker shoes to go as a teddy boy," he said tersely. "And his suit."

"Wow, good for you. Argh, is that the time?' She gave a very un-Charlie-like squeak. "Microwaves just beeped. Dinner's ready. Er, was there anything else?"

"No, er, see you tomorrow?" He daren't say 'see you later.' She might say no.

"Sure, looking forward to it. Laters."

There was silence from her end of the phone.

Jake went in search of Lily. She'd know what was going on.

Only to be thwarted. She'd left already.

Jake got ready for the ball in a very uneasy mood. It was a 'sword about to fall' feeling. Where you were damned sure something wasn't as it should be, but not sure what that something was. Even his appearance in the mirror, with a very satisfactory mustache and his hair greased into a not-too-shabby quiff, failed to please him.

It wasn't right without Charlie.

"Bannerman, you're an ass," he said to his reflection. Thank goodness it couldn't answer him.

He wasn't in a better frame of mind when he set off to the hotel where the ball was being held. His next-door neighbor was going into his house as Jake walked toward the taxi he'd booked.

"Very dapper. Have a good time."

He nodded and left before he was asked any questions. Such as who was he going with and what was she wearing.

Charlie? He had no bloody idea and it was no one's fault but his own.

* * * *

"Are you sure this looks okay?" Charlie asked Lily for the umpteenth time. "Not too OTT?"

Lily inspected her from top to bottom and sighed. "I wish I looked half as good. That dress is amazing."

Charlie smoothed the black-and-white pop-art '60s dress over her hips. "Gran said it was always her favorite." The dress and the Mary Quant cut-out tights had both been her gran's, as were the circular, orange plastic earrings. Even the shoes Charlie wore were authentic. White, faux leather, pointed, dinky stiletto heels. "I'm so chuffed I can fit into her stuff. It's strange, though, because I never saw my gran as 'with it.' She's the one who I always thought of as a prude and not interested in fashion. Then when I mentioned the ball and the theme to Mum over the phone, she told me Gran had lived and worked in London for two years, shopped in Carnaby Street and Biba's, which was the boutique to shop in. I wonder if that's where she got this Twiggy wig?" The wig in question was blonde and asymmetrically cut and covered all of Charlie's own red hair. "It just goes to show."

"If I wore my gran's stuff I'd be arrested," Lily said with a giggle. Her forays in the charity shops had found her hippy dress, forehead thong — a strip of thin plaited leather that tied round her head — and cowbell. A full-on hippy outfit, right down to the roman sandals, which tied up her legs. "She's four inches shorter and at least a size smaller. Her pelmet skirts would be a belt on me."

"I bet Terry would like that."

"Yeah, but Mrs. Macklin wouldn't, and isn't she on the door or something?"

Lily rolled her eyes. "Bit pot, kettle and black, that. Hypocrites 'R Us."

"Sadly."

"Anyhow, let's away and get jiggin'," Lily said in broad Glaswegian. "Or at least get our coats on and wait for Terry, who promised me no Marcus in the car. He'll meet us there and we're making a big group up."

Thank god for that. Charlie might want to go and ignore the fact Jake was going without her, but not rub the fact she was there with someone else in his face. Even if it was all window-dressing.

For the first time she began to look forward to the evening ahead. Damn Jake and his arsy attitude. He was a fantastic lover, the best tutor a newbie could wish for. Kind, considerate and innovative. Sometimes she marveled at how she had changed over the past few months.

From a not interested, can't stand cocky blokes virgin, to a what? Eager to learn, got a fantastic lover who was also—usually—her best friend. Okay, he blew hot and cold sometimes, but if she were honest, she hadn't been a lot better.

Until they had first made love.

Charlie accepted she'd fallen head over heels in lust. Which, she now acknowledged, had evolved into love. She had no idea if Jake felt the same. Sometimes she thought so, others that he was still at the deep-in-lust stage. Which was fine for now. However, Charlie was uneasily aware that soon it might not be. Love, if it was one-sided, wouldn't work.

She got into the back of Terry's car with a cheerful 'hi' and 'thanks for the lift.'

He responded with a whistle. "Got to have the camera handy when Jake cops an eyeful of you, Charlie."

She laughed. "Don't you dare."

"Never dare a dare-er," Lily said with a giggle. "He will, you know."

Charlie sighed. "Nothing to do with me if Jake goes apeshit then."

"Why should he?" Lily asked. "This is all his doing."

"Was that why he was threatening Marcus to keep his hands on his sporran if he didn't want his bal— Well, you know what I mean," Terry said hastily. "He got a wee bit worked up."

Sadly, that gave Charlie a twinge of pleasure. *My bad.*

"Ah, he'll get over it or not," Lily said with all the callousness of a sister. "He's had too much of his own way."

Charlie thought back over the last couple of months. She would have said they were even on who decided what. Luckily, in a lot of things their ideas meshed.

Except for this bloody evening. She should have stuck to her guns and refused to go.

"Stop at the shop, please, hon," Lily said. "I want some sucky sweets."

Terry groaned but pulled up outside the co-op. "I'll go in. What are you after, your usual?"

Lily nodded. "Please."

Charlie waited until Terry got out then asked a question that had been niggling her. "What time does this thing start?"

"About an hour ago, why?"

"Are we being fashionably late or what?"

Lily sniggered. "Oh deffo the 'or what.' I wanted Jake to get there first and wonder what's going on. Usually it's the other way around. Time to buck the trend, eh?'

"Lily Bannerman, why?"

"He's had it too easy. He loves you even if he never says so. He's different with you. Less up himself, less sure and much more likeable. This dance thing is an affectation now. A habit. And it's time he realized how it feels to wait and wonder. Enough already."

"You are evil and if it all backfires, remember whose idea it was. I'm not getting involved in that scenario."

"That's okay, I'll just blame Terry."

"Oh no you won't." Terry got back in the car. "You're on your own there, love."

* * * *

Jake tried not to look toward the hall door as it opened again. Still no Charlie. Was she even coming?

The music started up again. The band for the evening was a local group who specialized in '60s music and they were bloody good, even if they did stray into the '70s on occasion. He was damned sure no one cared as they thundered from *I Wanna Hold Your Hand*, and *Hi Ho Silver Lining*, into *Bad Moon Rising* then *Honkey Tonk Woman*. As the union café had echoed to hits of the sixties for the last month, most people knew the songs and were up on the floor dancing and singing at the tops of their voices.

"Dance, Jake?" Mairi stood so close it was uncomfortable. He took a tiny step back. She was one of the miniskirt brigade and her top was so low Jake wondered how she could breathe and not become topless. It did nothing for him.

Now if it had been Charlie...

"No thanks, Mairi."

Mairi pouted. "If you're looking for Charlie, she's not coming," she said in a spiteful voice.

Jake narrowed his eyes as he turned to look at her properly. "And you know that how?"

Mairi shrugged. "She said she wasn't going to hold... Well, anyway, why should she? Now that you've got what you wanted, you'll not be interested in her."

"Who says I have, and who says I won't?" Jake asked in such a harsh tone it was Mairi's turn to take a step back. "Listen good, Mairi, I know you don't like her. That's your prerogative. But if I find you've been feeding her lies, or spreading malicious rumors, also known as lies, you'll wish you'd never opened your mouth. And, I wasn't going to say this again or so forcefully, but fucking well back off. You are not my type. Bloody end of. How many times do I need to tell you? I've tried to do it politely, but enough is enough."

Mairi bit back a sob. Jake ignored it.

"If I find out you have had anything to do with Charlie not turning up, or coming and feeling awkward, you'll be advised to keep well, well away from me, Mairi. For a long time. I'm not sure I'd ever forgive you."

Mairi looked stricken, her eyes wide and her lashes wet. "I only... Why *not* me?"

He felt like a heel, but he was so bloody angry he had to bite his tongue and count to ten before he replied. "Mairi, I just don't fancy you. Sorry, but that's how it is."

"And you do fancy her."

"I do." That was putting it mildly.

Mairi sighed. "I think I've been a cow, as well as an idiot."

Jake nodded. "So do I. And only you can sort that out." He turned on his heel and walked to the door where he collided with Charlie coming in.

At least he thought it was Charlie. His mouth went dry when he looked at the blonde wig, blue eye-shadow and pale, pale lipstick. "Whoa, go you."

Behind her, Lily gave him a thumbs-up.

He blinked, rocked on his heels and smiled. "At last. You look bloody fantastic, Charlie."

She opened her mouth to reply and he swooped. Put his tongue between her lips and meshed it with hers.

Then kissed her as if his life depended on it.

Which, in one way, it did.

Someone whooped, someone hollered and there were several whistles.

When he drew back, lightheaded and hard-cocked, she was the one to blink. "If that's the sort of welcome I get for being late, I'll have to be late more often."

He grinned. "Please don't, my nerves won't stand it. Say bye-bye to the lovely people."

"What?"

"Wave."

"Oh, er, right." She waved. "Bye-bye, lovely people…"

Chapter Ten

Charlie found herself tripping as she did her best to keep up with Jake. "Slow down, I'm not used to these shoes."

Jake glanced at her feet. "Damn, sorry. Like 'em, though. Okay, hold on."

The world swayed as Jake picked her up and walked swiftly to the door. One of the lecturers opened it with a grin "Forgotten something?"

Jake shook his head. "Remembered something. My lady and I need time together."

"Then remember the uni rules," she called after them. "Official and unofficial."

"Rules?" Charlie asked as they made their way to the car park. She shivered. "My coat's still inside."

"Rules. No improper behavior on the premises—i.e., no sex in the uni grounds, safe sex elsewhere. That's the gist of them. Text Lily later. She'll get it for you. There's a blanket in the car. And my padded jacket."

Charlie wondered if she ought to pinch herself. She'd been certain the evening was going to be somewhat different from this reality. She was supposed to be at the Christmas Ball, showing Jake she wasn't bothered they weren't together, not in his arms on her way to goodness knows where.

"You can put me down now."

"No need. Almost at the car and you'd freeze." He crossed the frosty car park toward his car. "Fish in my pocket for the keys."

"You just want me to feel you up," Charlie said as she did as he'd asked. "Here you go."

"The 'feeling me up' is a side benefit," Jake said as he clicked the remote and the locks opened. He put Charlie onto the passenger seat and grabbed the blanket from the back seat. "Here you go. This lives in here in the winter, 'just in case,' as my mum says. She drilled it into us years ago to make sure there's one in all our cars since the time she and Dad got stuck on their way home from Glasgow and they hadn't got anything warm except for a couple of new bath towels they'd bought. She vowed after that we would all carry a blanket."

"Sensible mum, but what about you?" Charlie tucked the blanket over her and gave thanks Jake's car didn't have leather seats, and that once he switched on the engine they could be heated. Her shivers slowed down, and her teeth stopped chattering. "We can't share if you're driving."

"I've got my jacket, and I'll put the seats on."

Within a minute he'd done that. "Happy to go to the bothy? We need to talk and that's probably the best place."

"Fair enough, as long as it's warm."

"Sure, no problem." Jake started the car, and within seconds the seat began to warm up. Charlie wriggled to make sure all her bum welcomed the heat. Heated seats were something new since they'd moved to Scotland and to her they were one of the best inventions ever.

"Text Lily," Jake reminded her as they headed back to their village. "Though I'm sure she will have guessed."

Charlie nodded and sent the details to her friend who replied with one word—'enjoy'—and a winking emoji. She laughed and put away her phone. This 'tell a friend' most things was something new, and she really enjoyed it.

Jake glanced at her. "What's funny?"

"Your sister telling me to enjoy myself with you. Do you ever tell her to enjoy herself with Terry?"

By the light of the car's dashboard, Charlie saw Jake blanch.

"Hell no. I try not to think about it, for god's sake. She's my little sister."

"By how much?" She knew Lily was the eldest.

Jake shot a quick glance in her direction. "That's not the point. I'm six inches taller."

Charlie sniggered. "She's also around eight months older than me. Don't get into a panic. I'm old enough and confident enough to know what I'm doing. Which reminds me... The contraceptive pill."

"Yeah?"

"It's now considered to have been in my system for long enough to be effective. Not that anything is one hundred percent, but I reckoned I'd let you know." Charlie had thought long and hard about whether to share that information, but in the end had decided to. After all, Jake had been meticulous about using condoms, but, as many people could recite their horror stories about condoms that had split, she'd rather he knew there was extra protection in place. And if she were honest, she quite fancied seeing what he felt like inside her with nothing between them.

Jake drew up outside the bothy. "Shit, what a time to tell me. Now I'm bloody shaking and we need to talk before anything else." He got out of the car and walked around it to open Charlie's door. A courtesy she loved. "Let's get inside and get warm. Keep the blanket round you, I'll need to put the heating on."

As much as she'd like to say, 'you can warm me up,' Charlie didn't. She was doing her best not to let her teeth chatter. It was chilly.

It wasn't a lot better in the bothy.

"The heater's been on frost setting so nothing freezes, but that's not enough to keep us warm," Jake said as he shut the door behind them. "How about getting into bed?"

"I thought you wanted to talk? If we get into bed, the only talking will be of the 'ooohhh, yes, there, wow, more' sort."

Jake grinned. "True. Then I'll make coffee and we can do the blankets around us, Darby and Joan stuff, sitting in the chairs, not the curled up together, trying and not succeeding in keeping our hands off each other."

* * * *

"So what do you want to talk about?" Charlie asked as she nestled in one of the armchairs and snuggled under the blanket. The temperature was rising but not enough to risk shedding her cover. It was up to him now. She'd acquiesced and allowed him to bring her to the bothy to talk, so talk he better do. "I'm all ears."

Jake sat opposite her and turned his coffee mug around in his hands. "Hard to know where to start."

"Let's go for, why are you, at times, a prime up-yourself ass?"

He winced. "Ouch, why not say it as it is."

Charlie laughed. "Come off it, Jake, that's me being mild. Out of curiosity, why do you act such a jerk? You're good-looking and you know it, evidently women, if all the gossip I've heard is correct, fall for you, and you blow them off, often by text. No need, surely?"

He reddened. "Once, once only by text. And that was because she was out of the country and sending me texts and pics about her and the bloke she'd met. My looks are not down to me, and I guess good genes are hereditary. I…" He hesitated. "Shit, this will make me sound a right asshat, but it's a bit like a kid in a sweetshop. Take your pick, enjoy and move on. Goes to your head."

"Bleugh." Charlie made gagging noises. "Why am I here?"

"You're different. Okay, okay, don't make faces, it's true. I took one look at you and I was… She's for me. I wanted you. Not just in a sexual way, but in every which way. I knew I needed to know all about you." He ran his hand through his hair in a self-conscious way. "Why? No idea, you just hit me like a ton of bricks."

"So you behaved like a wanker."

He rolled his eyes. "Guilty, I guess."

Charlie threw the blanket off and went to sit on Jake's knee. "No guessing, Sherlock. You were. Now, though?" She wound her hands around his neck. "Now you're on the way to redeeming yourself. Just a few more questions I need answers to."

Jake groaned. "I thought there might be. Go on, hit me with them."

"Why the go alone to every uni activity? And the disappearing acts when you're there?"

He wrinkled his nose. It was so cute, Charlie gave in to temptation and kissed it.

"Tickles. What was that for?"

"To give you encouragement." She almost blurted out, 'because I love you.' That might be a step too far for him. "I'm all ears."

He grinned and moved her side to side over his cock. "I'm not."

"You are a..." She thumped his shoulder. His hardening cock rubbing against her was giving her very interesting ideas. "Nothing doing."

"Okay." Jake sighed. "It started a few years ago, when someone wouldn't take no for an answer. Not Mairi, and it's never happened since. This person, and I'm not naming names, told everybody we were going to the Spring Ball together. I think she thought it would force my hand. I'm not falling for that, so I went without her, and then asked one of my girlfriends—no benefits, not expected or wanted—to go outside with me for half an hour or so. And that, my love, is how legends are made. Last year I had no intention of going with anyone. This year I would have bucked the trend but you didn't give me a chance. I went on the defensive and did the big man devil may care crap. The rest you know."

"I'm glad you did your caveman act." Charlie swiveled around so she sat facing him. "It's better here than at the ball. Except...we need to decide how to pass the time. I have an idea."

"You do? What?"

"Last one naked makes up the bed."

Chapter Eleven

"So the idea is that we are going to celebrate Chinese New Year with a cooking competition, a five to enter and all monies to go to this year's chosen charity," Mrs. Macklin, the lecturer who had laughingly agreed to oversee the competition, said. "All entries will be tasted by a team of both students and lecturers chosen at random. Okay, coerced or blackmailed to be judges," she added to hoots of laughter. "All efforts will be judged without the judges knowing who cooked what."

The Christmas break was over, Charlie and Jake had spent as much time as possible together, sat the half-yearly exams — set to make sure they were on course for the final degree exams later in the year — and got used to the teasing about old couples or even odd couples.

Mairi had been incredibly subdued and had a tendency to walk in the opposite direction whenever she saw either of them.

" She's embarrassed, she'll get over it," Lily said.

"She'd better," Jake said as the three of them plus Terry did a tidy-up and clear-out in the bothy. "We're all on public transport next week—my car needs to go into to garage for some mechanical TLC. I wish one of you girls would pass your test."

"Not gonna happen," Lily said. "I'm not even thinking of learning. What about you?" she asked Charlie

Charlie shuddered. "I might be used to Hong Kong traffic, which is the pits, but the roads around here give me the heebie-jeebies. Once, just once, years ago I got behind the wheel of Mum's car. Legally, I've got a license but...no, not yet. Between their house and the nearest main road, which is what all of half a mile or so, I met three tourist cars, one of which was on the wrong side of the road, one which stopped dead with no warning, and one coming toward me, the driver of which, I reckon, thought he was doing the around Scotland rally. To say nothing of the itinerant deer that jumped out by a humpback bridge and the three pheasants who thought they ought to rule the road and meandered in front of me for a good hundred yards. No thanks, I'll flutter my eyelashes at Jake or take my life in my hands and suffer Duckman's." She did a very exaggerated eyeroll then sobered. "Seriously, do you really think Mairi will be okay?"

"She finally realized what a numpty she's been," Lily said with a chuckle. "And I think Callum Jack is showing some interest in her direction. She's always had a soft spot for him. Only time will tell, but it's share the bus or walk."

All of which was circulating in Jake's mind as they left assembly and headed to their various tutorials.

"So, little plum, are you entering something plummy?" he asked as he and Charlie headed toward the local swimming pool after their morning lectures. Both had a free hour and intended to spend it swimming. "Do you have plum pudding in Chinese cooking?"

"You have plum in sauce," Charlie answered him. "But if I enter, I'll more than likely do an old, tried and tested favorite."

"Which is?"

She tapped him on the nose. "Not telling. You?"

"I'll maybe enter, just to give you some heckling. It'll probably be chicken chow mein or chicken and rice." He paused as an idea hit him. "Fancy teaching me a recipe and we'll both cook it for the comp? Winner chooses where we go for our Easter trip." They'd decided to go away for a few days and were arguing amiably about where to spend the time. Jake favored Paris, Charlie the Isle of Skye.

"But if neither of us wins, how will we know whose idea we go for?"

"Get a committee of our mates to decide in a blind test. What do you say?"

"Why not, but not chow mein."

"Too difficult for you, my little plum?"

Charlie rolled her eyes, unperturbed by his teasing, which she now accepted as fondness, not contrariness.

"Nope. So which do you fancy cooking, Szechwan chicken or sticky duck? Both my mum's bastardized versions, so they're easy and the ingredients are in most supermarkets. I've got a great Peking duck recipe, but I'd have to head to the big Chinese supermarket to get the ingredients and I don't think anyone would wait long enough for it to be cooked. So, up to you."

"Which are you best at? Then we'll do the other one."

Charlie burst out laughing. "I'm good at both. Your call."

Jake took a deep breath. "Chicken." At least he had more of an idea how that should cook.

Three days later, he looked at the sticky, gooey mess on the plate in front of him and groaned. "How come yours looks ready to eat and mine ready for the dustbin?"

"You don't listen."

"You turn me on too much for me to listen, I just look at you and want to make love with you."

"Then you won't win. High heat means hot, low heat doesn't. Half a teaspoon means half a teaspoon, not whatever you throw in. Browned doesn't mean white or, alternatively, burned." Charlie sighed. "So throw it in the bin, and let's go and make love. A lot easier and a hell of a lot more enjoyable."

* * * *

Charlie shot a quick look at Jake and sighed. As ever, he'd approached his cooking as if he had to rush the goal or whatever they did in rugby. His chicken wasn't seared properly, his onions weren't softened or gently browned. His sauce looked like something you found in a used oil can and she'd bet the bamboo shoots her mum always added weren't cooked. As for his rice... She shuddered inside. He hadn't grasped the concept that a recipe was there for a reason.

"Two minutes," the lecturer who was acting as the invigilator, or whatever you chose to name her, called out. She wasn't one of the judges.

Charlie glanced around the hall. Six people had taken up the challenge and it seemed all, apart from her and Jake, were cooking noodles on the other side of the room, Lily looked up and winked. She'd gone for chicken noodle soup, which she said she liked, though not necessarily the way she cooked it.

There had been a few comments about Charlie having an unfair advantage because she once lived in Hong Kong, but, as Mrs. Macklin observed, that meant several other competitors would have the advantage if they did an Indian, Mexican or Spanish food competition. Even a Scottish one.

Charlie did her last, fast, high heat, stirring in of spices and began to plate.

Next to her, Jake swore and almost flung his offering onto a plate. "Make it tidy," she muttered out of the side of her mouth. They had been threatened not to help each other, or risk being disqualified.

"Time's up. Off you go." The lecturer sat down and began to write something on a sheet of paper.

"With you in a sec," she said to Jake. "Forgot to put my name under the plate." He nodded. "See you in the common room." It had been agreed they would congregate there for the decision.

Charlie stood back and waited until everyone had left and glanced around. The lecturer had disappeared into a storeroom, and she was all alone.

Good.

Two minutes later she left the room and made her way upstairs to the common room.

Jake hugged her as she went in. "Sorted?"

"Hope so. How long is this gonna take, do you think?"

"Long enough so we miss economics?" Marcus, one of Jake's friends, said. "I'm so not in an economical mood today."

Jake hooted. "Is that 'cause you've got your eye on those new rugby boots?"

Marcus shrugged nonchalantly. "I plead the fifth, or whatever you say."

Charlie laughed. "I'm missing Mandarin, but when I said it was to try and cook a Chinese dish, the lecturer said as long as I sent him my recipe in Mandarin characters that was as good as a full-on class. I did and he gave me an A. Let's hope my food is as good, but I'm not holding out. It went wrong as I plated it."

Jake glanced at her strangely. "How come?"

She shrugged. "No idea, but that's sod's law, isn't it? Where do you think we'll be going to over Easter?"

He pinched her cheek. "No idea, little plum, but it looks like we're going to find out soon." He inclined his head toward the door where Lucy Millen, a lecturer who wasn't on the judging team, stood.

"They've made their minds up, and ask you to go back down into the staff room so they can give you their comments first. Then you'll all head to the main hall for the winner and runner-up to be announced. After that they'll open the cookery room up to everyone to look or taste."

"I feel like I'm off to the dentist," Jake said. "A filling at least."

Charlie laughed. Her hands were clammy. "Root canal for me."

"Urgh. Ah well, soon be out of my misery," Jake said. "I did the 'try to make it pretty' like you said, but even pretty can't cover horrible food. The one thing I know I did do well was cook the chicken. Well, probably cremated it, but at least no one will get salmonella from tasting it."

Charlie hugged him, uncaring of where they were. "That's got to be a positive then." She took a deep breath. "Here goes."

To spare too many blushes, and to the everlasting thanks of all the contestants, the fact it had been decided to announce the judging and comments to the six contestants first meant a lessening of pressure. Charlie followed Jake into the staff room and twisted her fingers together. Nervous was an understatement.

This was it.

"Runner-up…" Mrs. Macklin announced and grinned. "I could do with a drum-roll, but you'll just have put up with me saying dah dah… Lily Bannerman. Well cooked, not quite enough flavoring, but tasty."

Lily gasped and held her hand in the air in a victory salute. "Yee-ha, go me. Wow."

The others laughed. Charlie looked down at her hands and wondered if she could bite her nails.

"First… imagine another dadadah drum-roll…" Mrs. Macklin paused dramatically. "Jake Bannerman. A family affair here, it seems."

Jake's mouth dropped open. "W-w-what? Me?"

"You," the head confirmed. "Well cooked and very tasty. Exactly the right amount of spice and well presented. Congratulations."

He turned to Charlie and hugged her. "I'll get the flights booked, but I can't believe it. What about you?"

She shrugged. "Not to their taste. Each to their own. Just as well we don't all like the same thing."

"So, if anyone else wants to know what we thought, feel free to come and ask. What with your fivers and other people's donations, we've got a cool three hundred pounds to go to the charities' committee. Now let's go and open up the cookery room."

Jake tucked Charlie's arm through his.

"We're on show," she hissed. "The decorum thingy is needed. Stop it."

"I don't think it'll matter today. Come on, let's go and see what's what."

"You go on, I need the loo."

"I'll wait for you."

Dammit. Charlie nodded, resigned to going into the cookery room with him. She nipped into the toilets and washed her face and hands.

"Lead on," she said once she'd rejoined him.

And waited for the fall-out.

They were the last through the door. There were at least fifty students milling around. Jake dodged between them, accepting congratulations and a lot of backslapping. With Charlie's hand in his, he made his way across to the food tables and peered at the first-prize rosette.

"There's been a mistake," he said to Charlie. "Look, that's yours, not mine. Let's tell someone."

"Really? Never mind, just ignore it."

"I can't, it's yours."

"You *can*. Don't make a fuss."

Jake narrowed his eyes. "How could that have happened?"

"No idea."

"I hesitate to call you a liar, love, but if you were Pinocchio your nose would hit the wall. Why?"

"Why what?"

He bent so he could whisper in her ear. "Charlie Allsop, I love you, but I'm not accepting this. Mine was a train crash of a disaster and you know it."

"I love you as well. Oh, and your chicken *was* cooked."

"And not much else. Come on, let's do the 'there must have been a mistake.' As we were side by side there's a minute chance it was a genuine mistake, but I don't believe in fairies."

"Well, damn you, you should."

He laughed and cleared his throat. "I'm not that up myself — or so insecure — these days. Hey, everyone, listen up. Somehow two name sheets got mixed up. That gorgeous one isn't mine. It's Charlie's. Mine is the mess no one wants to touch. I can't say I blame you."

* * * *

Three days later

"Here's the tickets," Jake said and handed Charlie a slim packet. "You look after them, I'd probably lose them on the way home." As he'd once left his new iPad on a bus because he wanted to reach the chippy before it closed, it could well happen. "What do you think? Timing okay?"

Charlie opened the packet and glanced at the contents, then dropped them on her lap and looked up at him uncomprehending. "I thought we were going to Paris?"

"Only if I won. Anyway, I've managed to book up into the Three Chimneys for one night. Posh nosh and all that. The other three nights it's an Airbnb. I haven't been to Skye for ages so I'm looking forward to discovering it all over again. This time with the love of my life." He kissed her and she reciprocated with fervor until they were both panting. "I love you, Charlie. Whatever happens in the future, I hope that's okay and tough if it isn't."

He began to unzip her jeans. Charlie wriggled to give him a helping hand as she used her fingers to toy with the zipper on his denims.

"More than okay." Charlie cleared her throat. "I know we're only youngish, I know we both have years before we're established in our chosen careers, but I also know I love you, and whatever happens in the future, I'll never regret any of our time together." She grinned.

"Unless you stand me up at a ball."

Want to see more like this?
Here's a taster for you to enjoy!

Sensory Limits
Ashe Barker, Elizabeth Coldwell, Wendi Zwaduk, Tori Carson, Zoë Mullins & Fara Allegro

Excerpt

Excerpt from 'Yes or No' by Ashe Barker

Martha sipped her herbal citrus tea, her nightcap of choice when she wanted—needed—to get a decent night's sleep. The pungent aroma of lemon and apricots teased her nostrils and the tart heat slid down her throat. She clasped her mug between both her hands as she read the advert again.

It was a reputable online fetish site, one she used often. She occasionally interacted with others in the community there, but most of all she valued their absolute discretion when she needed to do a spot of shopping. She had bought things from time to time and they always arrived in the post packaged in respectable brown cardboard. Her collection now ran to a vibrating butt plug, a couple of electronic toys, lube and on one occasion, she had splurged on a rather splendid G-spot USB-rechargeable rabbit vibrator. It had proved a tad awkward when she'd tried to take that particular item through the automated baggage check at Manchester airport on her way to Ibiza, but the security guard had been very polite about it. He'd wished her a nice time and re-zipped her case for her.

She grinned, remembering. She *had* had a nice time — plenty of sun, sand and solitary orgasms in her five-star hotel room overlooking the Mediterranean. But that had been over six months ago and she hadn't had a sniff of any action since. It was true she had been busy with work, but that was no excuse, not really. Her battery-operated boyfriend sat unloved in her bedside drawer along with her other fetishy bits and pieces.

Martha yawned, the herbal tea doing its work well. She shut down her laptop, set her empty cup aside and settled herself against the pillows.

It was only an advert, but a girl could dream.

As she lay, floating in that half-conscious existence between sleeping and waking, Martha rehearsed — and not for the first time — her own ideal sexy fantasy. She visualized the man — it had to be a man, she'd determined — who was a massive part of the turn-on for her. Her Dom would be a stranger or someone she did not know well. He would be handsome — of course — stern and demanding but not cruel. And he would be knowledgeable. He would know a woman's body better than she herself did. He would understand her responses. Everything he did to her would be deliberate, controlled, purposeful. She would be helpless, vulnerable but utterly safe in his expert hands.

Excerpt from 'Cruise Control' by Elizabeth Coldwell

Daniel surprised me with my present as I sat eating breakfast in the conservatory. "Happy birthday, darling." He pressed a kiss to my cheek and set a plain white envelope in front of me.

"Thank you." I'd been dropping hints about the stunning diamond earrings I'd seen in the window of the jeweler's shop on the high street, so I tried to hide my disappointment as I placed my coffee cup back on the table. Using my butter knife, I slit open the envelope. Inside was a printed sheet of paper. I glanced at it, realizing it was some kind of travel document. Once I'd skim-read it, I cast my gaze up to Daniel's handsome, impassive face. He was the master of giving nothing away. "This is a…cruise ticket."

"That's right."

"Wow, I don't know what to say." Of all the things Daniel could have bought me, this was the most unexpected. I only wished it was more welcome.

"I thought it would be nice to have a few days away. After all, when was the last time we took a holiday together?"

I considered his question for a moment. "I don't remember, unless going up to Edinburgh for your sister's wedding counts." He shrugged in a way that suggested it didn't, and I went on. "But why a cruise? You know how I feel about those things. They're what you do when you've retired — when you have the time to spend a couple of weeks doing nothing but ballroom dancing, playing bingo and watching awful cabaret nights hosted by some comedian who won a TV talent show thirty years ago."

"This won't be like that, Lily. It's a three-day trip down the Seine to Rouen and back. And there's an option to spend an evening in Paris. We could have dinner in an intimate little bistro or wander along the riverside by Notre-Dame. The city is so beautiful when it's lit up at night."

A stop-off in Paris, I had to admit, did sound romantic. "I suppose that isn't so bad." I glanced back to the ticket. "But this says we're scheduled to depart this evening."

"That's right. So hurry up and finish your breakfast, because you have some packing to do."

Immediately, my thoughts raced to what I'd need to take with me — and not just in terms of what I planned to wear. This would be the perfect opportunity to catch up on a couple of manuscripts that needed to be assessed.

As if he'd read my mind, Daniel added, "And no taking any work on this trip. This is all about us, not our jobs. Understand?"

I nodded and popped the last bite of croissant into my mouth. He might have won this round, but he wasn't going to get his way for the whole weekend. I was sure of that.

Excerpt from 'Just You and Me' by Wendi Zwaduk

"So many playmates, but not the one I want," Ryder muttered as he read the personal ads on the bulletin board. If he were writing his own advertisement, he would've said something along the lines of *Wanted — a lover and a sub who can handle me. Same woman preferred. Must be willing to work with me, but rein me in, too.* He snorted as he gazed out at the people in the main playroom of Exposed. The guests and members were great people, but in his six months there, he hadn't found the right sub. Well, no... He had an idea of who he wanted, but he hadn't had the chance to talk to her.

He leaned against the bar and toyed with his bottle of water. Just thinking about Cat sent the blood rushing below his belt. The sweet woman with the long blonde hair came to mind often. He wanted to caress her curves and sample her mouth. He'd heard she was into pain play and he'd watched a couple of her demonstration scenes. She turned him on and had him ready to combust each time he saw her. If she'd participate in a scene with him, he'd show her a good time. Hell, he'd show her she might be a good match for him, too.

Damian, one of the other Masters, strode up to him. He nodded once. "Ryder."

"D." Ryder stood tall. He hadn't been at the club as long as Damian and was expected to defer to him. "How are you?"

"I'm fine," Damian said, "but I've got a problem. There's a writers' group coming in at seven and they'd like a demonstration. One of the authors set it up with Sean, but the bastard left last week. He never bothered to let the group know that he wouldn't be able to do the demo."

"What does it involve?" He finished his water.

"Wax play. I don't do that with Missy." Damian notched his chin in the air. "You're not coupled up. I'd ask you, but you don't have a sub."

"I can find one." He knew who to ask. "Pencil me in for it." He left the empty bottle on the bar. "I'll do it."

"You're sure?"

"Positive." He clapped Damian on the shoulder. "We'll be there."

"I should ask who you've got in mind, but I trust you," Damian said. "I'll have the playroom prepped. Playroom one. The supplies will be there and ready. All you have to do is show up. Is there anything you want in particular?"

"I'll text you once the sub agrees."

"Good."

"Thank you." He left the Master at the bar and headed toward the office. He'd wanted an excuse to speak to Cat and now he had one. He ignored the others in the room. Right now, the only one who mattered was her. A woman in a latex dress winked at him. He nodded once, but kept moving.

"But, Master," she said, "I've been waiting for you."

He frowned. He wasn't even sure who she was, yet she'd waited on him? "I'm sorry. I'm not looking for a sub right now."

"Sir." She reached for him, but he sidestepped her. Besides her not being Cat, he wasn't in the mood for someone so pushy. He ducked into the hallway leading to the office and paused to compose himself. He had to think before he spoke. If he demanded her submission, Cat wouldn't work with him. He knocked on the door.

"Come."

Excerpt from 'His Lucky Day' by Tori Carson

Kat had been methodical in her preparations. She'd researched Stephen until she knew his weaknesses, then she'd devised her plan. Ever since she'd met the tall ex-Marine at the Association of Fish and Wildlife Agencies — AFWA — annual meeting, he had become an obsession that she couldn't afford at this point in her life. Her time was precious. With her doctoral thesis deadline fast approaching, she needed her wits about her. Instead of focusing on her paper, all she could think about was the firm jaw and challenging eyes of the local fish and game bureau chief.

In the agency's parking lot, she leaned against her truck's fender and went through her checklist one last time. Everything was accounted for. A smile lit her face. Twenty-four hours from now she'd have her life back.

She'd met his type before. Their confident swagger and hint of intelligence usually hid one of three things — a misogynist, a braggart or a bore. All she needed was to find which category to file the sexy man in, then she'd be able to concentrate again.

She stuffed the list into her pack and entered the lobby.

"Good morning," the receptionist greeted Kat.

The perky blonde with her sun-kissed waves held in place by a thick hairband set Kat's teeth on edge. *So the man likes a bit of eye candy in his office. Strike one.* "KT Riley to see the bureau chief."

Eye Candy's perfect smile disappeared as her mouth formed a hard line. "I'm sorry, ma'am. I don't see you on Dr. Andersen's schedule."

"Could you please let Stephen know I'm here? I only need a few minutes of his time." She didn't know him well enough to call him by his first name. They'd only spoken a few times, but she could repeat each conversation almost word for word. His deep baritone voice had a way of reaching inside her and curling her toes.

"One moment." The blonde spun her chair around and headed deeper into the office.

Kat couldn't hear the receptionist but she could understand Stephen clear as a bell. "About five foot eight, brunette, green eyes?"

He remembers me.

"Let her through."

It took a bit of doing, but Kat maintained a professional mask as Miss Eye Candy led her into the bureau chief's office. As soon as she entered, he stood and reached out to shake her hand.

"Ms. Riley, this is an unexpected pleasure. How can we be of service?"

"It's good to see you again, Dr. Andersen." She couldn't help but notice the way his hand engulfed hers. She wasn't a demure woman by any stretch, yet next to this man, she felt petite and feminine. It was distracting.

"We don't stand on ceremony here. Please call me Stephen." He waved her into the chair opposite his.

Excerpt from 'Bound to Happen' by Zoë Mullins

The line at The Mudhouse was out the door. For the first time since Jaymie and her best friend had opened the little café six months ago, she was convinced it was going to be a hit. It didn't hurt that it was crazy-hot out and they were offering large iced coffees for only two dollars a cup.

The crowds were larger on the weekend when the *city* people from Toronto drove up to their cottages on the lake. Even though she had studied in Toronto and forced herself to work there for a few years, she would always be a townie and proud of it. She hated the city, hated the late hours she'd put in at the magazine, resented the commute from downtown to the suburbs where she'd lived with another graphic designer and two additional roommates.

She'd been biding her time, skipping the parties and the clubs and saving her pennies until she could move home to Port Ellis. That she'd opened a coffee shop and bakery was entirely an accident of fate. It had been her best friend's idea. Mel'd had the know-how and Jaymie'd had the capital. After finding what Mel called the perfect location, it had all fallen into place with ease.

The Mudhouse was located on Founders Street, the town's main road. The shop itself was, to put it plainly, a hole in the wall — or maybe a closet. The coffee bar and bakery case were on one side with a row of tables against the other wall. The front of the café was also wide open to the sidewalk, with doors that could be retracted for the summer. What had convinced Jaymie that the location would work was the large deck off the back. It was the width of their shop and half of the florist's next door and had direct access to the boardwalk.

"You've done a good job at reinventing yourself here," Mel said, passing her a cup of iced tea.

"You mean co-owning a café when I neither bake nor drink coffee?"

"Ssh, we aren't telling the townsfolk about that. We'll lose the true coffee aficionados if they discover you scorn them."

"I don't scorn them or the coffee," she insisted, sipping her mango-pomegranate iced tea. "I just don't worship at the altar of the bean." They served a large selection of fair trade organic coffees, but Jaymie had made sure they also had the largest tea selection in Port Ellis.

"You don't know what you're missing." Mel took a large gulp of her iced coffee.

They leaned against the back railing, watching as their well-trained staff moved people through the line quickly. Their pastries were all homemade. That was Mel's passion, and while it would be better if they had a commercial kitchen on the premises, her partner seemed content to bake at home. Jaymie hoped they might one day be able to take over the florist shop next door and turn it into the kitchen of Mel's dreams, but that was a long way down the road.

As director of finance, Jaymie was well aware of their fiscal realities. She also handled their human resources and marketing needs—all roles that did not require her to get up at the crack of dawn. She was not a morning lark.

Excerpt from 'Black Ice' by Fara Allegro

Dear DareToSpankMe.com,
I challenge you to find me a plus one for Saturday night.
I have two VIP tickets to the sold-out Rocks Off gig in Hammersmith. Unfortunately, the lady I bought them for now prefers my best friend's brother. Her loss... He's personality deficient and allegedly even less exciting in bed. I'm on the band's after-show party list — equals two karma wins for me.

Can someone save me from a solo show? Or hitting the bar like a sledgehammer?

Amusing, interested replies encouraged — extra points for banter. Who's game? I'm waiting and my wallet's ready for the bar tab.
#freeticket #notastalker #RocksOffChallenge
Username — BlackRunSkiFreakDom

* * * *

I'm Jaye Ripley and it started with a slippery Dom's dare.

Yes, I know how bad that sounds. I usually only lurk on the spanking site and had never dared to interact before. But it was one of those stupid moments when your brain should opt for prudent sanity but said 'fuck it' instead. I blamed the open bottle of red wine and my inner speed-freak going on a bender.

I should've turned off the laptop and diverted my attention. But Mr. BlackRunSkiFreakDom was too enticing. Was it a line or was he for real? And why was my pussy tuned in to his wavelength, refusing to listen to reason?

He could be a serial Internet rogue with a scary record. But I'd been dumped without answers myself once. I empathized with his plight, so I posted my reply.

Hi, Ticket-and-Karma-Blessed Guy,

I'm a Londoner and I'm free on Saturday, so I'll be your plus one. Just don't expect me to fancy you. I'm off men forever and I'm so serious about it that I'm getting a 'No Men Zone' tattoo done soon. Pick me for the ticket and I'll send selfie proof.

I've also just filled in my convent application form. But before I go there, I'd like a last night of wild rock and banter. We both deserve a curtain call. Bring it on!

If this is a sympathy sex attempt, you are so not going to score! And I mean that.

#RocksOffCrazy #whatamIdoing?

Username – DaringSassyManHater

P.S. I am honestly off men – and I know karate!

Twenty minutes later, he'd messaged my site account. My heart galloped when I clicked on his BlackDom address line. He told me we were on and asked me to bring along karate belts. *Nice touch!*

BlackRunSkiFreakDom said there had been a hundred and seven replies. Mine passed on good punctuation. I'm a college English lecturer. Then again, maybe he was lying and I had been the only idiot to answer?

To think that I lecture students about avoiding risky situations… But, to date, my patented 'always be sensible and say no to fun' technique hasn't worked. And I was going to take three mobile phones for safety.

Sometimes thrill-seeking feels risky but right. My wish for a fantasy date with a mystery Dom was finally granted.

Home of Erotic Romance

Sign up for our newsletter and find out about all our romance book releases, eBook sales and promotions, sneak peeks and FREE romance books!

About the Authors

K.V. Rose

K.V. is an author of dark romance living in Toronto. She enjoys iced coffee, writing villains, and everything in black.

Kori Blue

Kori Blue writes adult romance with an edge. In her stories, you'll find sharp, sassy women who know what they want… and strong, sexy men who've got just what they need.

Kori's stories often involve some kinky fun, and explorations of fantasies from the sinfully sweet to the downright dark and dirty. A Kori Blue book is guaranteed to pull you into a world of intrigue and intensity, with characters you'll love, and heat you'll never forget!

Raven McAllan

An Amazon-bestselling, multi-published author of erotic romance, Raven lives in Scotland, along with her husband and their two cats — their children having flown the nest — surrounded by beautiful scenery, which inspires a lot of the settings in her books.

She is used to sharing her life with the occasional deer, red squirrel, and lost tourist, to say nothing of the scourge of Scotland — the midge. As once she is writing she is oblivious to everything else, her lovely long-suffering husband is learning to love the dust bunnies, work the Aga, and be on stand-by with a glass of wine.

These authors love to hear from readers. You can find their contact information, website details and author profile page at https://www.totallybound.com